COCKY

SUIT

D1607819

HARLOW LAYNE

COCKY SUIT

COCKY HERO CLUB

HARLOW LAYNE

COCKY SUIT

Cocky Suit is a standalone story inspired by Vi Keeland and Penelope Ward's Stuck Up Suit. It's published as part of the Cocky Hero Club world, a series of original works, written by various authors, and inspired by Keeland and Ward's *New York Times* bestselling series.

1

PRIA

SQUARING MY SHOULDERS, I HELD MY CHIN HIGH AS I opened the door to the office of the man who wanted to take the jobs of hundreds of employees. What he didn't know was that I didn't plan to leave until I convinced him to let every single one of the people at Gainsworth Investment keep their jobs.

Coming out of the bathroom, I saw the bane of my existence, Kingston Avery. He was tall, a few inches above six feet. His ten-thousand-dollar suit fit him as if it was made for him and I was sure it was. Blond hair fell over his forehead and his green eyes looked down as he tucked his semi-erect cock back into his pants.

He had no idea I was in the room until I squeaked and quickly turned around to face the door.

"What the fuck are you doing in here?" his baritone voice boomed.

"I'm your four o'clock. Ms. Wang." I turned and looked around the room to see if we were alone. Was there a woman hiding in the corner or in the bathroom?

"Wang." He said my last name like a stupid frat boy hearing the word fart or balls and snickering at it. His lips twitched and then thinned out.

I narrowed my gaze at him as his laser-like green eyes tried to eviscerate me. I'd never seen a man with eyes that looked like a frosted emerald. "I think you've got a little left-over dribble on your slacks."

He didn't look down. Instead, he stalked past me out to where his secretary sat. "Ms. Brooks, can you tell me why the fuck you let someone walk into my office without announcing them?"

"Um…" From that one word alone I could hear the fear in her voice.

"You're fired," he spat out before slamming his office door. My straight black hair blew into my face as he walked by. I tried to discreetly pull it out of my lip gloss while simultaneously wanting to run from his wrath. "Sit," he growled out.

I wanted to tell him to fuck off. Kingston Avery had no right to take his anger out on me. I mean what on God's green earth made him walk out of the bathroom with his cock in his hand when I came in?

I did as he demanded, though, because they always say you catch more flies with honey, and I couldn't let down the hundreds of people who were counting on me to keep their jobs once the takeover was over.

"Why did you ask for this meeting?" He looked down at my hands lying in my lap and raised an eyebrow with a sexy smirk. "Ms. Wang?" A smirk I wanted to slap off his gorgeous face.

I studied him from across his desk. Kingston Avery looked like the drop-dead gorgeous next-door neighbor with chiseled cheekbones, full lips that made you want to feel them, for them to touch every inch of your skin and plump enough to nibble on, and a strong nose. But it was his cold green eyes that let you know he wasn't a man to fuck with. One wrong word and he could end your career and run you out of town.

I held my head high as I looked into those biting green eyes of his. I already knew this was a mistake. This wasn't the sweet boy who used to do anything for his sister. I didn't know who he was anymore, and it was obvious he had no idea who I was. Should I mention that we knew each other as children? Even though I felt it was impossible, I still had to try. "I'm here on behalf of all the employees of Gainsworth Investment."

"Let me stop you before you start, Ms. Wang." Again, he smirked as he said my name. Internally, I rolled my eyes. It was strange, one word, my last name, made him act so childish when he was known to be such a hard-ass. There was no way I'd let it get to me now. I was over being made fun of for having the name Wang since the time I started grade school. "While it's highly commendable that you think you have the power to change my mind, I regret to inform you that it's impossible to bring on the entire company of Gainsworth Investment. What you really should be concerned about is trying to convince me to let you keep your job."

I ground my teeth together. "Mr. Avery, how can you in good conscience fire an entire company?"

"I'm not firing the entire company, Ms. Wang." He arched an eyebrow. "I'm going to have you go through all the employees of Gainsworth Investments and anyone who's not up to par doing their job needs to go."

"Why me?" I squeaked out.

"Why not?" He leaned back and put his hands behind his head. "You're now the head of Avery Capital Holdings unless you don't want the job."

It took everything in me not to jump for joy in my seat. Instead, I tried not to let show how excited I was at the prospect. "How much would I be making?"

"Starting off, your salary will be one hundred seventy-five thousand dollars. How does that sound to you?"

4

Sounds like I'd be buying a new wardrobe for my new job. Mama like. Mama like.

"Any benefits?" Like your luscious lips trailing down my body.

"All the standard benefits of health insurance, 401k, one week of vacation, and a week of sick pay for the first year and two for the next, Ms. Wang. Is that satisfactory to you?" Kingston brought his elbows down on his desk and clasped his large hands in front of him, his long fingers steepled under his chin.

My gaze roamed from his fingers up to luscious lips and back down again.

Damn his hands were big. I wondered if he was big everywhere.

Pria, you need to stop yourself. You've got Haider at home waiting for you and he loves you.

"I think I can work with that, Mr. Avery."

2

KINGSTON

GRAHAM MORGAN, MY OLD COLLEGE FRIEND FROM Wharton, set down his phone and smirked as I took my seat on the other side of the table from him.

"It's not like you to be late, King. Woman trouble?" His lips twitched as he tried to hold in his laughter.

Unbuttoning my suit jacket, I leaned back in my seat and took in my friend. There was something different about him, but I couldn't put my finger on it. I waited to answer while a waiter filled my water glass and took our drink order.

"Something like that. I fired my secretary the other day and the temp agency keeps sending the worst candidates."

Graham lifted a brow. "You've had her since you opened your company. I feel like there's a story there."

I chuckled to myself. "You wouldn't believe me if I told you."

A wicked grin crossed his face. "Well, now you've got to tell me."

"You know how I'm in the process of buying Gainsworth Investments." Graham nodded. At one point, he was going to buy it, but after finding out he was the father of his dead ex-friend, Liam, and his ex-girlfriend, Genevieve's, child, Graham backed out. It was a lot for him to take in and when he decided not to buy, he wanted to make sure the right person bought the company, so he came to me. "One of the employees there asked for a meeting. I swear my secretary was trying to sabotage me from the get-go. I'm not sure why she made the appointment in the first place."

Graham's brows furrowed. "That's not standard. What did they want?"

"That was my thought, so I looked her up to see if I could get an idea about what she might want and possibly cancel. You know how I like to be prepared. That was my second mistake."

Setting down his water, Graham asked with his head to the side. "What was the first mistake?"

"Not canceling the meeting."

"So, what happened then?" Graham asked when I sat quiet for too long.

"She was—is the hottest woman I've ever seen.

Even photographed. She's a petite little thing but even from her picture you could tell she's feisty." I couldn't help but conjure her image up in my head as I'd done every day since she stepped foot into my office. The way her big brown eyes took me in from across my desk and the blush that crossed her cheeks, I was sure she was thinking about my cock.

"Why did she want the meeting?"

"For me to keep all the employees at Gainsworth. I'm not cold-hearted, but I can't keep every single one."

"Takeovers are never pleasant," Graham grumbled.

The waiter brought out our drinks, and we took a moment to order dinner before we both took a sip of our Macallan's.

"Did you hit on her and she turned you down? I mean there's a first time for everything." He smirked at me from behind the rim of his glass.

My eyes narrowed before my lips tipped up. It's not like he'd ever had a woman turn him down. Why was he giving me shit? "No, dickhead, she didn't turn me down. I can't believe I'm about to tell you this." I took a hearty gulp of my scotch and shook my head. "Just looking at her picture made my dick so hard I knew I needed to take matters into my own hands, or I wouldn't be able to concentrate during our meeting."

Graham's elbows came down on the table as he leaned forward. "What did you do?" he asked with laughter in his voice.

"What any hot-blooded male would do. I went into my bathroom and jerked off." And I came harder than I had since I was a teenager with the image of her playing on a loop.

"I'm not seeing what the problem is, King. It's not like you were in the employee bathroom rubbing one out and got caught."

"How many people do you think are cracking one off in the bathroom at work?" It had been my first. "Is that a regular occurrence for you? If so, I think you need to get laid more."

Graham leaned back and crossed his arms over his chest. "No, I've never done it at work, and I get laid just fine so no need to worry about me."

He'd never done it at work but I'm betting he'd done it somewhere questionable. I lifted my eyebrow in silent question knowing he'd never answer me.

Graham laughed and shook his head in answer. "Why don't you stop deflecting and tell me what happened?"

Finishing off my drink, I took a deep breath. "I walked out into my office tucking my dick into my pants and there she stood."

"What? Why?" He laughed out. He barely got the words out he was laughing so hard.

"Why what? Why was she in my office? Good question. My secretary let her in my office. She didn't even announce her. Hence, why Ms. Wang saw more than she bargained for."

"Maybe you're upset because she saw your wang wasn't so big after all." Graham laughed to himself.

"Not the case, asshole, and you know it."

"If you say so. Did you end up having the meeting?"

"I did. It wasn't as successful as she wanted, but I think I found the new head of my HR department."

"You're going to hire a woman you think is hot and gets you hard as the head of HR? I'm not sure that's a very good idea."

"You're probably right, but it's a risk I'm willing to take." Even if I have a hard-on all day while at work.

"Just remember not to whack off at work." Graham laughed and finished his drink.

Of course, that would be the moment our waiter brought our dishes to our table. He had a questionable look on his face but didn't say anything. "Can I get you anything else?"

I ordered another drink to try to forget the week I'd had at work. "I'll try to keep that in mind, but it's not like I'll be seeing her every day. I'm the boss. I don't do Human Resources."

"Oh, King." Graham shook his head. "I have a

feeling you'll be seeing her more than you realize." Holding his finger up, Graham pulled his phone out of his suit pocket and smiled down at it. After typing out a message, he put his phone down on the table and took a bite of his steak. "I'm going to have to cut our dinner short."

"Really? Trouble?"

Graham smiled wickedly at me from across the table. "Only the best kind."

"Do tell. I have to say, I've noticed you seem different tonight."

His brows furrowed. "Different in a good way?"

"Yeah, you seem happy. Lighter. It looks good on you."

Graham had always seemed happy even back when the rest of us were stressed out studying for exams at Wharton. The only exception was when Genevieve fucked him over, but whatever this was, it was more.

"When I came to you to take over Genevieve's company, we didn't get to catch up. We should make time every once in a while."

"I'd like that." After Liam Gainsworth died at an early age it made me realize I needed to seize every day as if it were my last and not take for granted the people who were in my life. I had a feeling Graham had the same epiphany. "You didn't answer what's got you like this."

"You'll never believe it." He smiled wide and tapped his finger on the screen of his phone. "I met a woman and settled down. She's the best thing that's ever happened to me."

"Wait, are you married?" My gaze went to his left hand and found it ringless.

"Not yet, but I do plan to ask her to marry me. She's it for me and she loves Chloe just as much as I do."

"After what happened with Genevieve, I never thought I'd see you settle down, but damn if it looks like that, maybe I need to think about finding me a woman."

"Maybe Ms. Wang?" He smirked before placing his credit card in the bill sleeve.

"I guess I can't convince you to stay for a cigar." I motioned to the bill.

"Not tonight. Soraya's waiting for me at my place and I don't want to leave her waiting for long." A gleam came into his eyes. I knew that look. He was thinking about his woman naked.

The waiter brought Graham's credit card back and thanked us before leaving us to ourselves once again.

"I'll let you get home to your woman." I stood and held my hand out for him to shake.

"What? I won't sit and shoot the shit with you and now I don't get a hug?" Graham joked before pulling me into a back thumping embrace. "Don't be a stranger, King."

"I won't." Or I'd try not to be. It was too easy to let work take over my life. I worked sixty to eighty hours a week lately. The only thing I did for myself was hit the gym each day and spend time with my dogs, but I knew I needed more. What that more was, I wasn't sure of yet.

3

PRIA

I DOUBLE FISTED MY COFFEE CUPS AS I STEPPED ONTO THE elevator. It had been a long week, and I wasn't even close to finished going through all the employee files of Gainsworth Investments. I had not so lovingly started calling them the "G" files. I hadn't seen the light of day since I started working here and I hoped that wasn't going to continue after I decided the fate of who got to keep their job and who didn't. While I didn't relish the task of deciding the future of so many people, I did love my new office with its amazing city view and the money. I was already fantasizing about all the hot new outfits I was going to buy for work. Outfits I had a feeling my new boss would greatly appreciate.

I leaned back against the wall as the doors started to close only for them suddenly to open again. In walked Kingston Avery in another ten-thousand-dollar suit looking like a god. He looked as if he'd gotten a full ten hours' sleep when I knew that wasn't possible. Every night when I left, his light was still on and today was the first day I'd made it to work before him. It wasn't fair for a man to look so insanely good. It was as if the gods themselves had molded him to perfection. I hated where my thoughts went when I was in proximity to him. I had a loving fiancé at home to remember, yet every time I was around my new boss, I forgot all about him. *Haider doesn't look like Kingston Avery.* No one looked like Kingston, and there wasn't a Kingston for everyone. Some of us had to settle for ordinary men instead in lieu of males who looked like Greek gods.

He nodded when he caught me in the corner half awake and stood on the opposite side. His large frame seemed to take up most of the space. Being closed in with him, I could smell his aftershave, cologne, or whatever it was, and it was intoxicating. I was sure women smelled it as he passed by and followed him around like lost puppy dogs. You didn't even need to see his face or body; he smelled that good. There were probably a dozen of them standing at the front of the building now wondering how they got there. In that instant, I wanted to catch a cold or develop allergies so I wouldn't be lured in by his scent. It could only lead to trouble.

Kingston cleared his throat and when I looked

over at him, one brow was arched devilishly. "How's the new job treating you, Ms. Wang?"

"I… It's coming along. I feel like I missed something. A—"

"I asked you twice how the job was going. Was I wrong in appointing you as the director of Avery Capital Holdings HR?"

"No, not at all, Mr. Avery. I just haven't had my coffee yet." I held up the two cups. "I'm useless without my morning coffee."

"And here I thought you were bringing one of them for me."

His chuckle was gravelly and smooth all at the same time making me hate him all the more. I looked down at my two cups trying to decide whether or not to give one to him when his large warm hand, touched my arm. Sparks ignited and traveled from where he touched me all the way up to the nape of my neck.

"I'm only joking, Ms. Wang. I guess I don't have a sense of humor in the morning without my coffee, but don't worry, I don't plan to steal one of yours. I was going to make one in the employee lounge. Did you know there's a Keurig and a cappuccino machine in there?"

I didn't, otherwise, I would have saved the trip and avoided then line at Starbucks.

"No, sir. I didn't." I couldn't help but notice how his green eyes lit up when I called him sir. Did Kingston Avery like his women to call him sir in bed?

Stop thinking about him in bed, Pria! Remember, Haider?

He smiled showing his perfectly straight white teeth. "Do you see something you like Ms. Wang?"

"Just fantasizing about drinking my coffee once I get to my desk."

"That must be some damn good coffee you've got there." He grinned as if he knew damn well I wasn't thinking about my coffee.

He really was a cocky suit.

"Does the elevator seem to be going slow this morning?" I felt heat rise up my body, all the way up to the tips of my ears. I desperately wanted him not to notice, but from the gleam in his eyes, he'd caught it.

"Really? I hadn't noticed. I've been enjoying my time with you this morning." He smirked. "I'll have my assistant call down to maintenance to have them check it out."

"Good." I nodded and instantly felt stupid. Why did he get me all out of sorts whenever he was near? He was probably thinking he should have kept Wanda as the head of his HR department instead of me.

ALL DAY, AS I READ THROUGH THE LAST FOURTH OF THE Gainsworth Investments employee files, I couldn't stop thinking about my ride in the elevator that morning with Kingston Avery. From his mega-watt smile to his intoxicating scent, I wanted to be stuck in that slow elevator again with him instead of trying to decide if someone deserved to keep their job or not. Ninety percent of the employees at Gainsworth had nothing in their files to warrant their impending unemployment. They were great employees, many of whom had never even taken a sick day until Liam Gainsworth's death, which was surprising. Then there were the last ten percent that I wasn't sure how they'd managed to keep their jobs. When I worked at Gainsworth Investments Human Resources, it wasn't my job to oversee them, but now that I'd read through their files, they'd all be looking for new employment as well as the director of HR with Kingston's takeover.

I was a little nervous that once Kingston saw that I'd fired Ben Raider, the now unemployed head of Human Resources at Gainsworth, he'd want me back over there. I didn't want to have to show my face after deciding the fate of so many of my previous coworkers. Over at Gainsworth I didn't have a nice office with a view, nor did I have the amazing coffee I sought out in the early afternoon after Kingston had mentioned it. I hoped that he saw how hard of a worker I'd been since he'd hired me and would keep me around.

Haider: What time are you going to be home tonight? I'm going to make you dinner since you've been working so hard.

At least someone noticed.

Pria: Is an hour good?

Quickly I cleaned up my desk so I could get home and enjoy dinner with my sweet fiancé. I didn't realize until I was on the train home to Brooklyn that Haider had never texted me back. Maybe an hour wasn't enough time for what he had planned for dinner and he was busy trying to get it ready in time. It didn't matter to me. It was the thought that counted, and I was happy I didn't have to pick anything up once I got off the train. I'd help him if I wasn't a disaster in the kitchen. Everything I touched turned into a burnt crisp or a soggy mess.

Stepping onto the platform, I breathed in the crisp fall air. After being on the train for nearly an hour it was nice to take the fresh air into my lungs and catch a glimpse of the setting sun. After another moment of taking in the beauty surrounding me, I hightailed it to the house I'd shared for the last two years with Haider, ready to relax, eat dinner with my him, and let him relieve all the tension that had built up since I started working under Kingston. Not *under* Pria. For Avery Capital Holdings.

The moment I stepped inside, the scent of garlicky goodness invaded my senses. My stomach growled as I circled the couch and headed into the bedroom to find Haider. Slipping off my shoes and setting them in my closet, my toes wiggled and dug into the plush carpet, happy to be free from the confines of my heels as I made my way into the bathroom. I spotted Haider washing himself through the steamed-up shower door and watched him for a moment. His thin body barely took up space in the shower and I knew if Kingston was in my shower, he'd take up every available inch.

I closed my eyes, shook my head, and took in a deep breath as I tried to get the image of what my boss would look like in my shower.

"Pria?" Haider called out with confusion lacing his tone.

Opening my eyes, I saw him peeking out with his brows dipped low.

"You're home," he stated as if he was surprised I was actually standing in our bathroom. "What were you doing?"

"Thinking," I muttered as I turned around and walked out of the room. I couldn't tell him I was imagining my boss in our shower. Maybe if I wasn't sex deprived, I wouldn't be fantasizing about

Kingston day and night. Tonight, I would get laid and it would be the end of me thinking about my boss in ways I shouldn't.

Heading to the oven, I opened the door to see if dinner was almost ready right as the timer went off. I pulled the baking dish out and sat it on top of the oven as Haider wrapped his arms around me and kissed the space between my neck and shoulder. Placing my hands over his, I leaned back into him before I turned around to kiss him.

I stared up at his dark brown eyes that used to look at me with so much love but now seemed to look right through me. I didn't know how to describe it. All I knew was that something was wrong. Maybe Haider was more upset than he'd let on about all my long hours. One thing I knew, he wouldn't complain when my paychecks started to roll in. Well, he might when he saw all the new clothes I planned to buy this weekend after I got paid. I hadn't been able to spend my first check since it needed to go toward bills and my half of the mortgage.

"Dinner looks and smells good. I can't remember the last time I had a homemade meal. Thank you for cooking."

"No problem." He smiled, but it didn't meet his eyes.

"I'm happy to be home to spend the night with

you." I tried to appease him for being gone so much lately.

Pulling away, Haider started to dish the garlic ginger chicken he'd made onto our plates. I was hoping for Italian, but I should've known Haider wouldn't make it for dinner. He only ever made Chinese food. Growing up, I thought my family was traditional, but Haider's put ours to shame, with the exception that he made me pay for my half of the expenses and that we lived together before marriage. I'd been informed once we were married, I would no longer be expected to pay for anything. I had a feeling he and his family thought I'd quit my job and stay home. I knew I'd need to bring it up before we got married, but I didn't want to fight with him.

Without looking at me, Haider took our plates to our dining room table which he'd already set. He sat at one end and I at the other in total silence. I wasn't sure why we couldn't sit in front of the television and eat if we weren't going to talk. We used to talk about our days or what we wanted for our wedding as we ate dinner, but now my fiancé sat across the table from me without even looking at me. He stared at his food as if it was the most interesting thing in the world, and it took everything in me not to whip out my phone and scroll through social media. Instead, I sat in silence with the only noise being the scrape of our forks against the plates. Couldn't we have music playing in the background? I liked noise. Even at work, I had music playing or was listening to an audiobook through my headphones. Who had time to read an actual book nowadays? Certainly not me.

After rinsing the dishes, putting them in the dishwasher, and cleaning up the mess Haider left in the kitchen, I found him in the living room on the couch channel surfing. Sitting down next to him, I placed my head on his shoulder and wrapped my arm around his waist, snuggling close to him.

"What are you in the mood for tonight?" His voice was hoarse and strained, but I thought nothing of it. Maybe he was tired, but I had an idea for a way to wake him up.

No time like the present, my hand slid down his chest and glided down to his slacks to his zipper. My nimble fingers started to undo his button when Haider placed a hand on top of mine. When I tried to continue to the promised land, he peeled my fingers off one by one before setting them down on the couch between us.

Sitting up, I looked up at Haider with wide eyes. "Not tonight, Pria."

"If not tonight, when? I can't remember the last time you looked at me with lust in your eyes or wanted me to touch you."

Haider looked at the television and then back to

me, his face devoid of all emotion. "I said, not tonight. It's been a long day and I'm tired."

Biting my bottom lip to keep myself from crying, I stood from the couch. If Haider was going to turn me down, I was going to take care of myself.

4

PRIA

HITTING THE BLUE BUTTON ON THE KEURIG MACHINE IN the employee lounge, I patiently waited for the machine to brew my cup of coffee. I'd become a regular, drinking as many as five to seven cups throughout the workday. As luck would have it, a large yawn overtook me the moment Kingston walked in looking like a Manhattan god in a suit worth more than my entire wardrobe, his blond hair perfectly coiffed, and full lips tilted up as he chuckled.

"Long night?" One lone brow rose.

Instead of answering, I narrowed my eyes at him as the last drop of caffeinated elixir dripped into my cup. Lifting it to my lips, I blew over the piping hot liquid before taking a sip. It took everything in me, with him standing in front of me, not to think about all the dirty thoughts I had of him last night as I used my shower head to get off. It was too easy, and I didn't want to be like all the other women who watched him walk down the halls picturing him naked. I didn't blame them, but I had a fiancé. A wonderful fiancé who loved me and wouldn't break my heart the way Kingston Avery broke women's hearts left and right—if I went by what everyone in town said and the office gossip.

"Ms. Wang, cat got your tongue?" he said lasciviously with an arched eyebrow. How could one lift of a brow be so sexy?

"More like sleep deprivation," I clipped back. *And lack of sex.*

Kingston cocked his head to the side before taking a step forward. Plucking my coffee cup out of my hands, he set it down on the counter and gave me a once-over. It didn't feel sexual. *Like I wanted.* It was clinical. Assessing.

Heat rose up my body, and embarrassed by my blush, I turned to look down at my cup of coffee letting my long hair fall in a protective curtain around my face.

"You've been working long hours and deserve a break. Why don't you take the rest of the day off and don't show up until nine tomorrow? I'm used to being the first one here and the last one to leave until you came along. It's like you're trying to make me look bad."

How much of a life could he have working all the time?

Turning back around to look at him, I placed my hands on my hips, and tried to keep my voice level. "Are you doing this so you can fire me?"

"Fire you? You're one of my best employees." He paused and I thought for sure there would be a cocky as hell look on his face, but instead, he looked sheepish. "Before you took over as head director of Human Resources, I was informed that our policies needed to be amended for sexual harassment. I need you to read over Avery Capital Holdings' policies and update them. Once you're done, they need to be sent out to all employees at both Avery and Gainsworth. Can you do that?"

I was amazed at his faith in me. It would have taken me years and a big *if* for me to become the head of HR, but he must have saw something in me. *He* gave me a shot and I would do my all not to disappoint him.

"Yes, Mr. Avery. I promise I won't let you down."

"See that you don't, Ms. Wang." For the first time, when saying my last name, Kingston didn't say it with any sexual connotation, and he tipped his head to me as he walked out of the room. "Have a good day."

WITH A SPRING IN MY STEP AND ITALIAN TAKEOUT IN MY hand, because I was still jonesing for the carbs I didn't get last night, I opened my front door with a smile on my face. I was happy to be home early and surprised to see Haider's car out on the street when I walked up. My mouth opened to form my fiancé's name, but it died when I saw my fiancé with his pants down, his white ass bared to me as he thrust into a leggy redhead and she moaned his name on our kitchen table. It was a train wreck that I couldn't tear my eyes away from.

Never once in our three years together had Haider showed me one ounce of the passion he was entrusting on this woman. I watched as his hands cupped her voluptuous breasts as he kissed up her curvy frame. Seeing him touch her like that brought out all my insecurities of having tiny breasts with a petite body. In all truth, I looked like a pubescent boy when I was naked. I tried to make up for it by always wearing beautiful dresses and high heels and always having my hair done with a full face of makeup.

I'm not sure how long I stood there in shock. At some point my food fell to the floor, but I didn't feel it slip from my fingers and they sure as hell didn't notice as they continued to fornicate on the table, we'd eaten dinner at last night. I must have made a noise—or maybe time had slowed, and it was the sound of the bag of food hitting the floor—because both their heads swung in my direction with looks of shock on their faces.

Time sped up as my emotions caught up to me in a blinding rush. Suddenly, I was enraged as this hussy tried to cover herself as I stormed past them. The only thing I knew was that I couldn't stay here any longer. I had a strong feeling this wasn't the first time Haider had cheated on me. Not that it mattered. There was no way in hell I was ever taking him back.

Grabbing my suitcase out of the closet, I threw in everything of mine that was in reach as tears slipped down my cheeks. As I dumped the contents of my lingerie drawer, Haider walked in with this head down unable to look at me. At least he had his pants on. Otherwise, I might have gone all Lorena Bobbitt on him.

Grabbing my arm, he tried to stop me but I ripped it from his hold. "Pria, it's not what it looks like." His voice was so quiet and without conviction, he had to know there was no way I'd believe him. It was almost five months ago when he started to pull away and three since we'd last had sex. Now I knew why. Haider had been sticking his dick in someone else. The same man who wanted to wait to have sex until we got married and I had to beg and seduce the fuck out of him for him to finally give in eight months into our relationship.

"Please don't be a cliché, Haider. I don't believe

you tripped and fell, magically making your pants fall down, and impaled her with your penis. I must have walked in at the exact right moment. Or is it something else? Because I'd love to hear how this isn't how it looks." Heading to the bathroom, I grabbed another bag and swept everything on the counter into it. I didn't care whose it was. I didn't ever want to come back if I didn't have to.

"Just look at me for a moment and let me explain." He grabbed my arm again and this time I let him turn me to him. I let him see the tears and devastation on my face. Haider pulled in a breath as if it hurt him to see me broken. What was he expecting? "You're too smart and deserve more, so I won't disrespect and lie to you. I wanted to tell you last night. I thought you'd come home late and…"

Oh, now he didn't want to lie and disrespect me. Good to know. Maybe he should have thought about that before he dipped his wick into that cesspool between her legs.

Pulling away, I continued to pack my belongings. I had no idea where I was going, but I wasn't going to show up at work tomorrow looking like I went on a bender the night before or worse. "And what? Start a fight with me and break up with me? That still wouldn't have been honest."

Sinking down to the floor, Haider looked up at me. Did he really need to get comfortable to tell me his story of infidelity? Why did he think I wanted to hear how he cheated on me? "About six months ago Kiki joined the firm, we met and fell in love." Looking down at his lap, he shrugged as if it wasn't a big deal. As if he hadn't wrecked my world.

"As easy as that," I sniped out. I wanted to stab him or at the very least kick him in the balls. I couldn't imagine if the shoe were on the other foot, he would be as understanding if I stated that I met someone at work and we fell in love.

"As easy as that," he repeated. "I didn't want you to find out like this."

"I doubt you would have wanted to walk in and find some guy balls deep in me," I gritted out as I continued to pack the rest of my stuff. Squatting down, I retrieved my vibrator from deep underneath the counter. I didn't bother to hide it as I securely put it in my bag. It couldn't get damaged now that I had no hope of getting any real dick in the near future.

"What's that?" I kept my back to his confusion. Of course, he wouldn't know what it was. I wanted to stick it up his ass and turn it on, but I refrained. There was no way I was giving Haider the satisfaction it had brought me over the years. Whirling around, I smiled. I knew it was ugly, but I was feeling quite ugly in that moment.

"It's my vibrator. You should probably invest in

one if you want to keep what's her name out there interested in having sex with you."

"What... what are you talking about? Why do you have one?" The confusion on his face was comical as his eyes bounced back and forth between my face and the vibrator in my hand.

Going back to finish packing, I fought back the laughter that was bubbling up in me. "I have one because I wanted to have an orgasm every once in a while, and it wasn't going to happen with you so..." I shrugged as if it wasn't a big deal.

Haider huffed from behind me but I paid him no attention. I wanted to get out of there as fast as possible.

"Pria." he sighed as he stood up. I watched him through the mirror. He looked sad, but he also looked relieved, which pissed me off.

Stomping out of the bathroom, I grabbed the handle of my suitcase and looked over my shoulder at Haider. "Were you going to ask me to move out last night?"

"I was hoping you'd offer once we talked and agreed *we* weren't working."

We weren't working because he was cheating on me. He all but encouraged me to work long hours night after night.

Rolling my suitcase down the hall, I glared at the woman who was standing in my kitchen with

Haider's button-up on and nothing else. "The reason we weren't working is because you've been sticking your dick into some red-headed hussy named Kiki."

"Really, Pria, there's no need for name calling." His voice was full of disappointment and I didn't give one single shit about it. Did he really think I was going to take the news that he'd been cheating on me for the last six months well?

"No," I whirled around on him taking him off guard enough for him to take a step back, "you should have said something the first time you fucked her. You should have moved out. You should have—"

"It's my house, Pria. My name is on the deed. You only pay minimal expenses," he huffed. He had no right to be angry with me.

Putting my hands on my hips, I glared at him for a moment before training my eyes on his mistress. Was it a mistress if we weren't married? I didn't care because it sure as hell felt like it. "He wouldn't hear of me paying for more and once we got married I was supposed to stop paying altogether. I'm sure he's made me out to be some horrible woman who wanted him to pay her way, but that couldn't be further from the truth. I wanted to pay more, but every time I mentioned it we got into a fight. You better watch your back with him." I jutted my thumb at my now ex-fiancé. "It would be wise to read up on traditional Chinese families. I can tell you one thing for sure. They will *never* accept you. You're beautiful and all, but you're not Chinese and they won't accept anything but a purebred."

I saw a light click on in her head before a wall came down and she blocked me out. Whatever. I didn't care. Let her get fucked over by Haider just as I had.

Making my way to the door, I shot back, "Enjoy his tiny dick."

5

KINGSTON

HANGING UP WITH MY MOTHER, I SIGHED HEAVILY. I hated to disappoint her, again, but there was no way in hell I was going to let her set me up with another one of her vapid friends' daughters. In the last year, she had decided it was time for me to settle down, find the perfect woman, get engaged (probably so she could plan our engagement party and our wedding), get married, and give her lots of blond grandchildren. It didn't matter that I wasn't ready nor did I find any of the women she set me up with remotely intriguing. My mother's grandmother biological clock was ticking, and she needed me to remedy it.

Throwing all the files I'd need into my briefcase, I closed it up, grabbed my cell phone, and slipped on my suit coat before I left my office. It didn't matter how big and grand my office was; being in it for sixteen hours a day was suffocating.

Seeing the doors of the elevator about to close, I jogged before I missed it and had to wait another five to ten minutes. I didn't own the building, but Avery Capital Holdings did take up the entire top floor. Since there was only one elevator in the building, I'd have to wait another ten minutes if I missed the current ride down. On most days it wouldn't be a big deal, but tonight I was tired, and I just wanted to pick up some takeout on my way home, eat, and then crash. It had been a long day and an even longer week as I got ready for an out-of-town business trip. Hell, it had been a long month if I was being honest with myself.

"Hold the door," I shouted when I saw I'd have to sprint to make it. I didn't have the energy to run. I barely had the energy to shout.

I saw a delicate hand hit the button for the doors to open, and I sighed in relief. Stepping onto the elevator, I turned to thank whoever had saved me from waiting. I wanted to be gracious and then go to my corner and wait until we hit the ground floor. All that changed when I spotted the new director of HR huddled on the other side of the elevator trying to pretend she wasn't there. Or at least that's what it looked like. Her long hair was down, hanging around her shoulders and acting as a curtain. After a moment, I noticed those slim shoulders of hers were shaking.

Maybe she saw me running for the door and was laughing at me.

Sniff.

Or maybe not.

My body turned to her fully now to see Ms. Wang standing there curling into herself. One hand held onto the railing that went around the entire elevator while the other hastily wiped at her face.

Taking a step toward her, I kept my voice low. "Is everything okay, Ms. Wang?"

Her only response was to turn toward the side wall and stare down at her feet. Okay, she didn't want to talk. I could understand that. I didn't particularly want to have a conversation either, but she seemed to be in distress.

I could handle just about every situation in or out of the boardroom no matter how stressful. The one exception was a woman crying. Growing up, my sister had been extremely sick. Almost everything they tried she was allergic to, so she was miserable, and in turn, so was my mother. Both would cry together for hours on end and I would have done anything to make them stop. Now, I had white knight syndrome, or that's what I'd been told it was called.

Sniff. I turned my head to the sound.

Sniff. Was she crying?

Placing my hand on her trembling shoulder, I

quietly spoke her name. "Pria." What I didn't expect was for Pria to turn around, bury her face in my chest, and start to sob. Gut-wrenching sobs that caused an ache in my chest. The only other people to ever cause that twinge deep in my soul was my sister, Murphy, and my mother.

Hesitantly, I wrapped my arms around her quaking frame. One hand rested along her lower back and the other held her head to me. Leaning down, I rested my cheek on the top of her head. "Is this about work? Do you hate it here?"

"No," she squeaked out. Her dainty arms wrapped around my waist as she snuggled in closer and continued to cry into my chest.

My hand slid down her silky black hair that went almost down to the middle of her back and up again. I continued to try to soothe her the best I could without knowing what was wrong. The only thing I knew was that she was the most beautiful, feisty, and unpredictable woman I'd ever met. I felt as if I knew her even though we were ever only ever together for a few minutes at a time, if that. Something about her spoke to me and I wanted to investigate it further even though I knew nothing could ever happen between us. There was a no fraternization policy at Avery Capital Holdings and as the owner and head of HR, anything we did would be a big no-no. We couldn't do anything, but I could dream.

Once every last shudder ran out of her body, Pria tried to step back, but I held her to me afraid she might start crying again. Placing her hands on my chest, she looked up at me with a tear-streaked face. Her mascara was smeared under her eyes and her nose was red. Even a sad mess, Pria Wang was beautiful.

"I'm so sorry. I didn't mean to break down on you, but I promise I'm better now." Her voice was slightly raspy from crying. This time when she tried to step back from me, I let her. My hands slid from her body and then fell to my sides.

"What happened? Did anyone give you a hard time today? An employee? Do I need to fire anyone?" I asked in rapid fire succession.

A small smile tipped her lips. "Nothing happened with an employee. I thought I was finally alone and could leave without anyone seeing me cry. I guess I was wrong."

I wasn't sure if I was relieved or not that it wasn't an employee. If it wasn't someone who worked at Avery then it had to be something personal and big. Pria didn't seem like the type of person who cried easily or for no reason.

Nodding as if this all made sense, I tucked my hands in the pockets of my slacks and asked her quietly, "Why were you crying?"

Pressing her back against the wall, Pria looked

down at her purple painted toes and wrapped her arms around herself as if she might fall apart again at any second. "Do you remember when you sent me home early yesterday?"

"Yes," I answered hesitantly. I never let anyone leave early, but I knew she'd been working long hours since she started here. That's why I couldn't understand why she was breaking down.

"I appreciate it by the way." Her tone said otherwise, but I let it go in the hopes Pria would tell me why she broke down on the elevator. "I left, picked up Italian, and went home. Color me surprised when I saw my fiancé's car in the driveway." She looked as if she was trying to chew gravel as she said "fiancé." "I was excited to be able to spend some time with him, but when I walked inside..." Pria gasped back a sob. Her brown doe eyes met mine. "He was fucking some hussy on our kitchen table."

Shocked, I leaned back against the opposite wall. I wasn't sure if my mouth was agape or not. One hand fiddled with the keys in my pocket as I tried to figure out what to say.

Cocking her head to the side, she mocked me. "Cat got your tongue?"

"I didn't know you were engaged, Ms. Wang."

Hands flying to her hips, Pria glared at me. "That's all you've got to say? If you had ever looked at my hands instead of my boobs, you would have seen the engagement ring."

My eyes went to her left hand that was sans engagement ring. "Well, in my defense, you've got great boobs."

"Oh please, I know what I've got." Her hands cupped her breasts and pushed them up. My dick twitched at the sight. He didn't care that the moment was inappropriate. "Give me something better than you've got great boobs." Pria looked around the elevator in a huff. "Is this the longest elevator ride known to man?"

I hadn't noticed, but we had been in the elevator for quite a while. "It does seem a little longer than normal."

Flailing her hands around like she was swatting at a bug flying around her, Pria stomped to the wall with the buttons and hit the button for the ground floor. "We could... I could have been on my way to nowhere," Pria uttered the last part on a cry. Her body started to sink to the ground, but I moved to grab her and sank to the floor with her in my lap.

"What do you mean you've got nowhere to go?" I asked into the top of her hair.

Situating herself on my lap, Pria got herself comfortable and snuggled into me. "I lived with my fiancé and now I've got to find someplace else to live."

"Where did you stay last night?"

She hung her head even lower. "A hotel."

I didn't see the problem with staying in a hotel. In fact, I'd stayed in one for weeks before. I was going to spend the next week and a half in one, and I didn't mind.

Noticing my hand on her knee, my index finger started to trace circles on her lightly pigmented skin. "It's usually affordable to live in a hotel for weeks and the accommodations are quite nice. You don't even have to make your bed if you don't want to. I can suggest some hotels I like to stay at if that will help."

Pria stood with her hands on her hips, and glared down at me. "Not everyone can afford to stay in a hotel for an undetermined amount of time, Mr. Cocky Suit, and there's no way in hell I'm going to stay with my dad and my Lao lao."

Disregarding her comment about my cocky suit—not knowing what the hell it meant—I looked up at her and it took everything in me not to smirk at the pissed off look she was giving me. "What's a Lao Lao?"

"She's my grandmother and to say we don't get along is the understatement of the year. I can't go there." She started to hyperventilate, shaking her head rapidly. "I've got nowhere to go. Nowhere. What am I going to do?"

Standing, I looked around the elevator for something to say and spotted a suitcase in the corner. Somehow, I missed it when I spotted Pria breaking down only moments after stepping onto the elevator. She really didn't have any place to go.

Clearing my throat, I walked over and picked up my briefcase. "Do you like dogs?"

Pria did a double take. "Um... yeah, I like dogs. Who doesn't?"

Plenty of people.

"I've got a proposition for you that will help you out with your problem and mine." I wasn't sure if what I was going to say was the right thing or not, but before I could stop myself, the words tumbled from my mouth. "Tomorrow, I'm headed out of town for a week and a half and I have three dogs who hate to be kenneled." Hate didn't even describe the amount of hell they put the last workers at the kennel through. "I need someone I can trust to take care of them." They can be a bit... much.

"Three dogs... and you trust me? Um, what..." Her big brown eyes looked over at her suitcase.

The elevator doors opened, surprising both of us. I liked our little elevator bubble and was sad to see it end. Walking over to her suitcase, I grabbed the handle and started off the elevator.

"Wait," she yelled. Turning around, I watched her

glide off the elevator as if the last few minutes hadn't happened. "Where are you going with my suitcase?"

Walking backward with her suitcase in hand, I shot back, "I'm taking you to my place."

Pria's eyes went wide. "What? Why? I'm not—"

Not wanting to hear her shoot me down even though I wasn't going to proposition her with sex, I stopped her. "You can stay at my place while I'm gone and take care of the dogs. Deal?"

Pria sputtered. "Your place?"

"Yeah, you'll have someplace to stay and can look for an apartment."

"You, Kingston Avery, are offering to let me stay at your apartment? Am I on *Candid Camera* or something?"

"Why not? I'm a nice person. Plus, you'll be helping me out. If you don't want to help with my dogs then I'll take them to the new place I was going to try. It's up to you."

"You're a nice person." Her tone said she, in fact, did not think I was a nice guy. Yes, I could be an asshole, but not when it came to my dogs. Ever since the takeover of Gainsworth, I'd been working extreme hours, neglecting them, and I felt bad. That's probably why they'd been acting out more than normal. If Pria agreed to this, she had no idea what she was getting into.

Stepping outside in the cool air, I noticed my

driver get out of the town car. He'd been waiting while we forgot to hit the elevator button. "Do you think I'm an asshole or something?"

Pria looked me up and down assessing me. "The verdict is still out."

Interesting.

Pointing at the car, I said, "That's my ride. What's your decision? Are you going to move into my apartment for the week? It's now or never."

6

PRIA

WHAT THE HELL WAS I DOING SITTING NEXT TO MY BOSS, pulling up to his place? I couldn't live in my boss's apartment for a week. Could I?

The building was one of the best in the city. It was in one of the nicest neighborhoods in Manhattan, and luxurious, but staying where he banged god knew how many women was gross. What I needed to do was get over myself, otherwise I was going to be living in my father's home with my Lao Lao, and I'd *almost* rather be homeless than listen to her nag at me about when I was going to get married. If she found out Haider and I broke up, she'd tell me that I was going to die alone, and it was all because I chose to have a job.

"Pria." Kingston brought me back to the here and now. His hand was on the doorknob as he looked down at me with… was that concern in his eyes? Maybe he wasn't an asshole. "Are you backing out?" The sexy smirk on his face told me yes, he was indeed an asshole, and I wanted to slap it off him.

Squaring my shoulders, I narrowed my eyes at him. "I'm not backing out."

"You should know about the dogs. They… well, they…" He looked confused and hot as hell while running his large hand through his ruffled blond locks as he tried to figure out what to say. I decided to save him just as he was saving me, and so he'd stop making his hair look sexier. I needed to repeat to myself not to have inappropriate thoughts about my boss.

"They're just dogs, and for a place to lay my head at night, I can handle anything you throw at me." My grip on my suitcase tightened as I took a step forward.

"Whatever you say, Ms. Wang." He drew out the *a* in my last name in a way that I knew he was thinking inappropriate or childish thoughts. Again, I wanted to slap him. How was it that I always seemed to want to slap him or jump him?

Kingston opened the door and held his arm out indicating I should go first. Okay, maybe he was a little bit of a gentleman. Wheeling my suitcase behind me, I walked into—I'm not even sure what you'd call it. It was not an apartment. I had only walked into the foyer and could see the living room, but the space was bigger than my entire house that I shared with Haider. The entire house. This was a palace in the sky on the top floor. The decor was all white, black, and gray—very bachelor. Everything was made of leather or metal, and it was all expensive and luxurious. What did I expect from a man who wore ten-thousand-dollar suits to work every day?

I was starting to turn around to express how lovely his home was and that it was not, in fact, an apartment when I swear the few pictures that were on the wall started to shake. It sounded as if a stampede was coming toward us. Slowly walking backward, I ran right into Kingston when two monstrous dogs came flying around the corner and jumped on me. One was on each side of me with their paws on my shoulders as they licked Kingston's face.

"All right." Kingston let out a deep belly laugh. "I missed you too. Now, Orvy and Sarah, get down. That's no way to greet a guest in our home." He gave them both affectionate rubs before pushing them off me. My back was plastered against his long, hard body and I didn't want to move. He felt too good. I'd take his behemoth dogs mauling me if it meant I got to keep my body pressed against his a little longer. Sadly, he broke the spell when his hands gripped my shoulders as he brushed his body against mine when he moved around me. I didn't think it was necessary, but I liked it, nonetheless.

Looking down, I spotted what would normally be a cute little dog, but it wasn't cute because it was humping my leg like I was the first woman who'd ever walked into the apartment. At least someone was interested in humping me.

"Jimmy." Kingston scooped the tiny dog up into his arms and I watched in utter fascination as the pup licked my boss all over his handsome face. Kingston smiled the whole way through before he said in a much higher voice, "I know she's pretty, but no humping our guest." Sitting the dog down, he took my suitcase from me and walked away. "I'll show you to your room and after I feed the dogs we can order in dinner and go over their care."

Dutifully, I followed behind him with my eyes wide and my mouth hanging open. It wasn't because his apartment was huge and incredibly decorated, even if it was typical bachelor pad décor. No, it was because no matter how many times I'd seen it at work, I hadn't realized just how phenomenal my boss's ass looked in his suit. We kept walking down the hall only passing by a few doors until we came to one at the end of the hall. How large was this place?

"This is your room. Feel free to put all your stuff

away." He placed my suitcase in front of the closet. "Is this all your stuff?"

"The rest is at the office. I didn't want to haul it around to wherever I ended up tonight. I'll bring the rest back with me tomorrow. It's not much."

"If you need any help, Roger, who's the day doorman, will gladly help you out." He looked around the room as if it was his first time in there. "You can do whatever you want, and I won't hear it. I'm on the other side of the apartment, but I guess it won't matter after tonight."

"You don't have to worry, I'm not a loud person."

"Is that so?" A large smirk crossed his chiseled face.

Internally, I rolled my eyes and acted as if I didn't get his innuendo. Was sex the only thing he ever thought about? It certainly seemed it was all I thought about when I was in proximity to him.

Leaving the room, Kingston looked over his shoulder at me. His eyes were dark as they scanned me up and down. "Put your things away and when you're done come out and help me decide what to have for dinner."

Had I entered the twilight zone? Kingston Avery was nice and caring, and dare I say almost... sweet?

Slipping my heels off, I opened the door to the closet and gasped. Holy hell, it was the biggest closet I'd ever seen. That seemed to be a running theme when it came to Kingston Avery. It was one of those closets you'd see in a magazine of a master suite. But never in a guest bedroom. Had Kingston given me the master suite? There was an honest to god island in the middle of the closet. An entire wall was meant for shoes. Never in my wildest dreams could I imagine the amount of clothes it would require to make a dent in all the storage. The best part about it was it smelled like cedar. I could spend hours in its little sitting room looking at how beautiful it was. If I lived here, I'd never want to leave.

Stepping outside the closet, I looked around the bedroom in utter astonishment. The bed seemed to be bigger than a king and yet barely took up any space at all. One wall was entirely made up of windows that looked out on what seemed to be the entire city. His apartment was like a mansion on top of a skyscraper. I'm not sure why I was so surprised. Kingston grew up with money and he made a hell of a lot of it on his own with Avery Capital Holdings.

After unpacking my meager belongings into the closet of all closets, I went out in search of my boss. I needed to keep reminding myself he was my boss and not the hottie that was currently standing in his kitchen.

I couldn't help but do my own appraisal of him as he'd done of me before he left me to unpack. He looked good in his natural habitat. Not that he didn't look good at work, but here in his home with his suit jacket off, hair in disarray, white shirt sleeves rolled up, and standing barefoot in his kitchen, Kingston Avery was phenomenal. The look of stress was no longer evident on his face, and as he smiled and played with his dogs, I wanted to run my hands through his hair and jump him.

"Everything okay, Ms. Wang? You're not still thinking about your tool of an ex, are you? Because if you are, let me tell you something. He was stupid to cheat on you. Stupid. Utterly stupid. I would never... Any man who would cheat on you needs his head examined."

"I... no I wasn't thinking about him." But I was now. Changing the subject so I wouldn't start crying, I asked, "Did you give me the master suite?"

Kingston along with all the dogs cocked their heads at me. He made a strange sound in the back of his throat as his lips moved with nothing coming out. "I gave you the biggest guest room. Do you want to move to a different room? It won't hurt my feelings."

"You have feelings?" I blurted out before I could stop myself. Slapping my hand over my mouth, I looked at him with what I was sure was terror in my eyes. I had to remember that even if I was in his home, Kingston was still my boss and I couldn't say anything I wanted to him or I might get fired.

A low rumbling chuckle filled the room. "On

occasion, I seem to exhibit signs of feelings." His eyes narrowed as his full lips tipped up. "If you tell anyone, I'll have to kill you."

"Under penalty of death seems pretty harsh." I moved into the kitchen to find about twenty menus laid out on the counter. "It looks like you do takeout as much as I do."

He looked down at the menus, one shoulder went up in a half shrug. "I work late and it's more fun to order for one person than it is to cook for one."

I didn't even have that excuse. I could have cooked for Haider and me, but after work and almost an hour ride home, I was in no mood to cook. Maybe that's why Haider strayed.

"What are you in the mood for?" I noticed then that the menus were organized by cuisine and at least half of them were Chinese.

I came around to stand beside him, so I didn't have to try and read them upside down. "Anything but Chinese."

Kingston leaned his hip against the counter, looking down at me. "I don't mean to be insensitive, but are you Chinese?" Immediately he looked away and I swore I saw the slightest tinge of pink in his cheeks. I had to be imagining everything about tonight because nothing made sense, especially my boss being embarrassed.

"One hundred percent." The bite in my tone was

unnecessary and I hated it immediately. I didn't want Kingston to think he'd upset me by his question. It wasn't him in the slightest. I couldn't stop thinking about the redhead I caught Haider with. From an early age, I knew I'd always marry someone Chinese because that was the way I was raised, and that's all I'd dated since I was allowed to start dating at the age of seventeen. That's not to say I wasn't ever attracted to a male of another race, but I was never interested until I stepped into Kingston Avery's office and saw the Adonis standing before me.

"I'm sorry. It's not you." I closed my eyes and tried to calm down enough to explain. "All my life I was brought up to believe that the only right man for me would be Chinese and my fiancé. Ex fiancé, Haider," I amended. "He was very traditional in most ways."

"Wait, your boyfriend's name is Haider?" He choked out as if it was the funniest thing he'd ever heard. He doubled over the counter. His low rumble of a laugh filled the space. "As in 'hate her'?" He placed an elbow on the counter as if it would help stabilize him from falling over. It didn't work. Kingston slapped the counter and pretended to wipe a tear leaking out of the corners of his icy green eyes.

It did kind of sound like that and I had to laugh along with him. It felt good to laugh today after feeling as if life as I knew it was over.

Straightening up, I turned back to the menus. Standing there with Kingston was a mixture of both awkwardness and comfort. It made no sense and yet it did which further confused me. "My ex only ever ate Chinese food." It never made sense to me since I'd grown up in a traditional Chinese family and although we ate a great deal of Chinese food, we ate other food.

Kingston started picking up all the menus that were Chinese and threw them in an empty drawer. "Do you have a drawer solely for menus?" I asked on a laugh. It was possible since his kitchen had more cabinetry than my entire house. *Not your house anymore.*

"It wasn't being used for anything else." He studied the menus as if he'd never seen them before. Was he embarrassed? Out of nowhere, he said, "How about pizza and ice cream?"

"That's random."

"What do chicks usually eat after a breakup?" Again he was looking down at me. Normally, I hated being so short at an even five feet with everyone looking down at me but not around Kingston. He had to look down at the majority of everyone he spoke to since he was so tall, and I didn't think it bothered him to peer down at me.

"How tall are you?" Dear God, did I not have a filter tonight?

Another low rumble rolled out him as he hunched down some as if he was trying to appear smaller than he was. Placing my hand on his chest, I stepped toward him. "Don't do that. I like how tall you are."

He licked his lips as his eyes turned from an icy mint to jade. "Do you now, Ms. Wang?" I was starting to like the way he drew out the *a* in my last name. And with that, I stepped back. I didn't need to do something I'd regret in the morning; I couldn't imagine having to work with my boss after kissing him.

I smiled and looked back down at the counter and the remaining menus. "Pizza and ice cream, it is. You'll get brownie points if you like pineapple on your pizza."

"Only if it's Hawaiian." One of the large dogs nudged Kingston's hand and he immediately started to scratch behind its ears. "Now that we have that settled, what kind of ice cream do you want?"

"Do any of the pizza places have ice cream or gelato?" I couldn't ask him to make two separate orders. He was already going well beyond anything I ever expected.

"Sure. Luigi's has gelato. Their banana is to die for." A moan slipped from his lips and I nearly fainted on the spot. Holy hell, I wasn't sure I was going to make it through the night without jumping him, especially if he made those kinds of noises.

"Banana it is." Maybe I was into torturing myself. "And who is this?" I pointed at the dog. I couldn't tell if it was a boy or a girl and didn't want to offend him. After all, I was here to watch his dogs.

"Right, what was I thinking? I need to introduce you. After that, we'll eat and I'll explain what you need to do while I'm gone."

The dog followed in step beside me as we trailed behind Kingston. It seemed more the size of a horse than a dog. What had I gotten myself into with agreeing to watch them? We stopped in what I would call a living room, but it seemed more like a movie room with how large the TV was. It had to be the largest on the planet. It seemed my boss didn't do anything small.

Turning toward me, he kneeled, and all the dogs went running toward him. Was that some sort of command or something, because if it was, I was never kneeling in front of them. "Pria, this little guy is Jimmy Chew. He humps just about anything." As if on command, the tiny brown and black puppy started to hump one of the beds that were on the floor. Well, now I didn't feel so special.

"This beauty is Sarah Jessica Barker." I did a double take on the name. *Sarah Jessica Barker.* Had I heard that right? She was adorable. She was all gray

57

even her eyes except for a spot of white on her chest. "Sarah, say hello to Pria."

Sarah lifted her head in the air and walked away. Okay, maybe not so cute. Seemed she had a bit of an attitude.

"She's a bit of a diva," he said with pure affection in his tone as he watched her walk away. "And this big guy is Sarah's brother, Orville Redenbarker, but I call him Orvy." Orvy's ears perked up. He too was adorable and didn't seem to be a diva. He had an intelligent face and knowing eyes. His were also gray, but he was white with black spots.

I plopped down on a comfy leather chair and started to laugh. I couldn't hold it in any longer. "Okay, I've got to ask. Where the hell did you come up with those names because seriously, Jimmy Chew, Sarah Jessica Barker, and Orville Redenbarker?" It took longer than it should to ask my question between my laughter. Those were the best dog names ever. Not that I'd tell him that. I needed to give him shit for it first.

In an instant, the happy-go-lucky guy was gone and in his places was the cold man who I was used to. More graceful than should be possible with his tall frame, Kingston stood. The ice was back in his eyes as he looked down on me. This time I didn't have the warm tingles. No, he wanted to eviscerate me with one look alone. "My sister named them before she died."

Silently I watched as he walked away with all his dogs following along behind him.

Maybe now wasn't a good time to tell him I knew his sister and his family.

7

PRIA

STRETCHING MY ARMS ABOVE MY HEAD, I OPENED MY eyes to Kingston's lavish guest room. It had been the best night of sleep in as long as I could remember despite the way things ended with Kingston and having found out that my fiancé had been cheating on me for the last six months. The bed conformed to every curve of my body. The sheets had to have been a thousand thread count. Hell, I had no idea how high of a thread count sheets could go, but whatever it was, Kingston seemed to have had them on his guest bed. Don't get me started on the plush comforter that felt as if it was snuggling up next to me and put me into a deep sleep almost instantly. Slipping out of bed, I quickly used the restroom and tried to make my hair look presentable by running my fingers through it before I left my room. I wasn't sure when my boss would be leaving for his trip and I didn't want to look like something from *The Night of the Living Dead* if he was still here.

Padding down the hallway toward the kitchen, I was met with six eyes staring back at me. I think we were all in shock as we stood there, unsure of what to do. I was beginning to think it was a mistake to agree to watch his dogs when I had no idea what I was doing. Especially when two of the dogs were bigger than me. How was I supposed to walk those beasts? Maybe they walked themselves. I had a feeling I was in for a rude awakening.

Before I could take another step, the dogs were running in the other direction. Instead of chasing after them, I followed my nose to the smell of some of the best coffee I'd ever smelled. One look at the coffee machine, if you could even call it that, and I knew I'd never figure it out. It looked like something out of a sci-fi film instead of something capable of brewing the magical elixir I needed every morning. I guess I'd be hitting up the nearest Starbucks on the way to the office.

Sitting next to an almost empty coffee cup, I saw a folder marked rules on it. Flipping it open, I thought for sure I had to be dreaming because there was no way in hell Kingston Avery expected me to do everything that was entailed on page after page of what seemed like a mini novel. I still hadn't figured out how I was going to take them out to go to the bathroom. Did I take them out one at a time or all at once? Maybe I could hire a dog walker to do that part. Why didn't Kingston have a dog walker? Was he an asshole to everyone and they all quit?

RULES

Don't let the dogs get up on any of the furniture. They each have their own beds in the living room and the master bedroom. Be firm with them and they will listen.

To do EVERY TIME before you leave the apartment:

•Food and water.

•Bathroom break.

•Put Animal Planet on TV to play in the background.

•Give each their own toys. There are baskets marked with their names.

DID THE DOGS ALSO PUT THEIR OWN TOYS AWAY? I HAD serious doubts about that one. How was I supposed to remember what toy belonged to what dog unless they only had one each, but I had serious doubts if they each had their own baskets?

BEFORE BED:

- •Bathroom break/walk.
- •Treat
- •Brush teeth.
- •Play with each dog for thirty minutes.
- •Turn on soft music/nature sounds for them to fall asleep to.

BRUSH THEIR TEETH? NEVER IN MY WILDEST DREAMS DID I think anyone was brushing dog's teeth. Was it too late to back out, because I couldn't imagine trying to force those big dogs mouths open and sticking a toothbrush in there? Did they have their own bathrooms too? Maybe if I was lucky, they peed in there. But according to the rules they were to be taken out to use the restroom. Still, I wouldn't be surprised to find they had their own bathroom with toothbrushes, shampoo, and brushes.

MAKE THEIR DINNERS IN THE CROCKPOT. IT'S IN THE cabinet underneath the coffee machine.

- •Monday - Chicken, rice, and carrots.
- •Tuesday - Organic Stew (see recipe in the drawer).

• Wednesday - Ground turkey with mixed vegetables.

• Thursday - Ground beef, potatoes, and green beans.

• Friday - Brisket

• Saturday - Ground sausage and rice.

• Sunday - Bake peanut butter treats.

THE NEXT WEEK MIX IT UP SO IT'S NOT THE SAME. You'll find the recipes in the back of the folder.

OKAY, NOW I KNEW THIS HAD TO BE SOME SORT OF A joke because there was no way in hell, he made their dinners every night in a freaking crockpot.

Kingston's icy voice grabbed my attention from this elaborate hoax. "I see you found the folder."

Seemed he was still upset at me. I had no idea that his sister, Murphy, had died. Once she was out of high school, my father was no longer her family physician. I couldn't believe he hadn't mentioned her death to me. I wasn't particularly close with the Avery family, but I would have given my condolences if I had known. Now, it was too late. I had always thought Murphy was a sweet girl. She had loved animals, but her parents wouldn't let her have one because she was sick most of the time and said she wouldn't be able to take care of it. Whenever I saw her when we were younger, I always tried to play or talk to her. Her mother always tried to shoo me away as if I carried the plague. Like my father would have brought me there if there was any chance I could have gotten Murphy sick. Still, I was saddened by the news. It made sense for Kingston to be upset by her passing. More than upset. They had always been close. Obviously, since he let his sister name his dogs.

In all truth, I loved the names, but in no way did I see Kingston calling them by those outlandish names. It just didn't seem his style. Neither did the idea he'd own a dog let alone three. I was already picturing dressing the little one up while he was gone. I wondered if there were any Jimmy Choo accessories for dogs. If there were, I was going to have to buy him something. Well, not me because there was no way I would pay that much, but I bet my boss would.

Holding up the folder, I turned around to face him. He was dressed in another one of his ten-thousand-dollar suits, navy blue, with black Italian shoes. His hair was slicked back, and I absolutely hated it. I wanted to run my fingers through it and mess it up, but I knew that was inappropriate and he didn't want me to touch him in the slightest if his laser green eyes were anything to go by.

"This is a joke, right?"

"I don't have time for jokes. My car will be here in a few minutes, so if you have any questions ask them now." The entire time he spoke, he kept his eyes on the folder. I wasn't sure how to get back on his good side or if he needed time to cool down. You would have thought overnight was enough time, but I guess not.

Are you over Haider cheating on you? That's not the same and you know it. And no, I wasn't over it. I wasn't sad anymore, but I was pissed. I wanted to go and slash my ex's tires, only he didn't own a car. He said we'd get one after we got married. Maybe he'd get one after he married Kiki, the hussy.

Not wanting to think about Haider being balls deep in that redheaded slut, I looked back down at the rules. Hell, these dogs ate better than I did. Did they really get homemade food every day? Did Kingston do all of this each day for his dogs or was he doing this because someone else was watching them?

Waving the papers in his face, I asked, "How can I do all this and work? Who does this when you're at work all week?"

"I had someone who came by in the afternoons and some nights to help with the dogs, but she was recently fired." His jaw ticked, and I had a feeling someone had done something to one of the dogs or him. I couldn't tell what, but I knew he'd been wronged.

"Did you go on a firing spree recently?" First his secretary, then the people at Gainsworth, and now the dog walker. I wasn't sure what to think. Maybe he went through employees like water and I shouldn't expect to have my job for long.

His nostrils flared as he shouldered by me over to the dogs that were patiently waiting for him by the couch. "It seems I needed to clean house. There were a few people that needed to go."

Okay, that didn't help me feel secure, but I'd let it go for now. He wasn't insinuating I would need to look for a new job anytime soon.

"I don't know much about dogs." Or anything really. "But don't they need to go to the bathroom more than twice a day? Is someone else coming to let them out during the daytime?"

"Normally, yes, someone would come during the day to walk them. I hadn't thought of that." He said the last part as if he was saying it to himself. His eyes brightened as if he'd come up with the best solution. Maybe it wasn't me. "You can work from home. I'll email IT when I get in the car and tell them to meet you at your office. Someone will put a program on your laptop that will make it so you can work while you're here. It's simple. I have it on all my computers."

He wanted me to work from home so I could take the dogs out? He either really loved these dogs or he was crazy.

"Is that all right with you, Ms. Wang? If there's an emergency, you can always go in and handle it. Do half days or whatever's easiest for you, but yes they need to be taken out around lunchtime."

"Um... I guess I can do that."

His phone buzzed from the pocket of his slacks. Kingston pulled it out and quickly put it back. "Good." He nodded as he made his way over to the front door. "I've already taken them out for the morning so they should be good until lunch." Picking up his briefcase from the side table and grabbing his suitcase, Kingston slowly looked me up and down. The only indication he liked what he saw was the darkening of his eyes. With one last look, he opened the door. "My contact information is in the folder if you have any questions." He gave me one final look over. "Nice pajamas, Ms. Wang. I hope I get the pleasure of seeing you in them again."

I stood there for a good solid minute unable to move after I watched him walk out the door. It should be illegal how good that man looked in a suit. Did he know how good his ass looked in those pants? I wanted to find his tailor and thank him for his outstanding work.

Finally, I looked down. I'd forgotten that I only had on a small pair of sleep shorts and a tank top that did nothing to hide my erect nipples. Why hadn't I remembered what I was wearing and put on a robe or a sweatshirt before I came out?

8

KINGSTON

I TAPPED MY FINGER ON THE CONFERENCE TABLE IN AN attempt to keep myself awake. My eyes struggled to stay open with each passing minute. Jet lag was real, and it was kicking my ass. I'd been going nonstop since I landed in London early this afternoon, and my day wasn't going to stop anytime soon it seemed. Ms. Sinclair, a leggy brunette droned on and on about the financials for her company and why they'd started to lose money in the last two years. I couldn't wait until she got to the part where she tried to convince me that Avery Capital Holdings could turn it all around for them if I invested in them. Sadly, it wouldn't happen today.

Looking down at my phone to check the time, I noticed I had an email from Pria. The time read it was six in the evening in London so that made it one o'clock in New York. The email was time stamped an hour ago asking about a three-headed leash. I wasn't sure if I should have been concerned by Pria's question or laugh. Why had I thought she could possibly handle the terrible twosome and Jimmy? Sarah and Orvy would kick her ass while Jimmy would happily hump her leg into next week.

"It seems we've lost Mr. Avery. I'm sure he's tired, so why don't we pick this up tomorrow morning after we let our guest get some rest." Ms. Sinclair smiled thinly at me. How long did she think she could hold my attention? They moved up this meeting by a week which had left me in desperate need to find someone to watch Orvy, Sarah, and Jimmy since I'd fired their previous dog walker. The agency had assured me that their customers' privacy was of the utmost importance and I'd believed them until I came home early one night to find Karen in my bedroom, naked, on my bed and rolling around. I'm still not sure if she meant for me to find her like that or if it was a regular thing she did after walking the dogs. Either way, Karen had to go.

Pria needing a place to stay was perfect, or it was until I saw her in her barely there sleepwear. I guess it was a good thing I was five hours away, I wasn't sure I'd be able to keep my hands to myself. It took all my control this morning not to strip her down and lick every inch of her smooth skin and pull her pebbled nipple between my lips. Instead, I left adjusting my cock before my driver thought I'd developed a crush.

Scooting my chair back, I stood to my full height and looked down at Ms. Sinclair. She was short but not nearly as short as Pria. Slowly her gaze traveled up my body until her eyes locked onto mine. She bit down on her bottom lip while batting her eyelashes at me and I wanted to roll my eyes. I'm not sure who told her that was the way to get a man interested in her because it did the opposite. At least for me. Throughout my life, I'd had women throw themselves at me for all the wrong reasons. For my looks or my money, but never for the man I was.

Did she really think I'd sleep with her just because she licked her lips and batted her eyes at me? I didn't mix business with pleasure. I'd learned long ago from my buddy Graham the dangers of sex and relationships in the workplace. Not that there was any chance I'd fall for the woman in front of me devouring me with her eyes. Desperation did not suit her and I needed to get out of there before she opened her mouth and I had to turn her down. That would only make the rest of my trip unnecessarily awkward. For her. I didn't give a shit. I was already counting the days until I could head home.

Putting on my fake smile and not giving a damn if she could tell or not, I picked my briefcase up from the floor and nodded to the room at large. "I'll see you in the morning."

The clicking of heels followed me out of the conference room. I ignored them as I leisurely walked in the direction of the elevators. I only hoped my jet lagged brain didn't steer me wrong to end up cornered by Ms. Sinclair. I could smell her desperation all the way from here.

"Mr. Avery, do you need a recommendation for dinner?" When I didn't stop or turn around, she kept going. "Or anything else?" Her voice went up on the last word. I wanted to turn around and ask her when prostitution became legal in England, but I refrained. See, I could be a good boy when it was required. But if she continued to try and get in my pants, I might have to rethink taking over the company. I didn't want to have to avoid her every time I was here on business.

"Ms. Sinclair, thank you, but I'm quite familiar with London. I'll see you in the morning to hear the rest of your riveting pitch." My tone let her know I did not, in fact, find anything about what she'd said today intriguing.

Her bottom lip stuck out like a child. This time I didn't bother holding back my eye roll.

"Very well. You have my number if you need it."

I wouldn't but I didn't tell her that.

Reaching the elevator, I hit the button down and

didn't look back. Once inside, I pulled my phone out and started to compose a message to Pria. It was obvious she had no prior knowledge of dogs, but I knew she'd try her damndest to stick by all the rules I'd left for her.

Instead of finishing my email, I decided it was probably best to talk to her in case she had any questions. Luckily, I'd had the forethought to put her contact information in my phone before I'd left town. My new secretary didn't seem to appreciate having to give me Pria's contact information. I'd seen her looking at me, but I didn't think she was stupid enough to act on her attraction to me. Most women found me attractive. I knew I was good-looking, but they didn't find my attitude toward them appealing and left me alone. Did she think if I had sex with her, I wouldn't be an asshole to her? Maybe I should have my head of HR remind the employees at Avery Capital Holdings that there was a no fraternization policy and that if someone did sleep with someone else at the company they would both be fired.

Dialing Pria, I started to walk toward my hotel. I'd been cooped up too much today and since the weather wasn't too bad, I decided to get some fresh air.

"Hello?" she answered breathlessly. "No, stay on the sidewalk."

"Pria, is everything okay? I got your message."

"Kingston... I mean Mr. Avery, um... yes, I believe everything is okay. I waited to hear from you, but the dogs really seemed to need to go outside. I know you're busy..." There was a muffled noise and then a loud squeak. "I was hoping for some direction on how to walk two... large dogs and one little one."

I had a feeling she was calling Sarah and Orvy something else in her head and it was most likely rightfully so. They could be a handful. I couldn't imagine someone as small as her trying to take them out. I really was an asshole for asking her to do this for me.

"You've got to show them who's boss. Say it like you mean it and they'll listen. They've all been to obedience school." I didn't mention how Sarah had flunked twice. She understood what you said, the problem was she didn't care. Orvy hated getting in trouble so he always did what he was told, and Jimmy went with the flow. He was pretty chill unless he was humping something.

"Okay." She didn't sound too convinced. "Maybe I'll watch some videos on YouTube tonight or something. Do you think it would be okay if I walked them one at a time until I get the hang of it? Me and poor Jimmy can barely keep up."

"That should be fine as long as you take them all out."

"I wouldn't leave one out." Her voice rang with offense down the line.

"No, of course, not." If I had an evil smile one would be plastered across my face in that moment.

Maybe I should've told her I usually held Jimmy after he'd done his business to make the process easier. I would give anything to see her right now. I'd bet anything it was comical as fuck seeing them pull her down the sidewalk like a rag doll.

"How many dog walkers do you usually have? I can't imagine only one person doing this every time. Now I know why you're in such great shape. It's from chasing after your dogs all the time."

So, she'd noticed I was in shape. Interesting. Things had been so hot and cold with Ms. Wang; I wasn't sure if she was attracted to me or not. Maybe she was just observant, but I preferred it if this wasn't a one-way street and she wanted me as much as I wanted her. Even if nothing could happen.

"As of right now, I only have you. Up until recently, I had a girl who did most of the dog walking."

"Are you sure it was only her. Maybe her boyfriend came with her to help out because unless she was a… some sort of mutant or superhero or something, I don't know how she did this. It's impossible." Pria sounded as if she was about ready to cry.

"Well, if you don't think you can handle it, I can

find someone else." Somehow, I knew she'd take the bait and wouldn't give up, and for some unexplainable reason, I didn't want her to. I wanted her to still be in my apartment when I got home from my trip.

"I can handle it," she hissed.

"Are you sure? You were just—"

"No, Sarah. No," Pria yelled out in terror.

Goose bumps prickled up my arms and the hair on the back of my neck stood. "Pria, what's happening?" I asked as calmly as I could as I stood in the middle of the sidewalk. I didn't care about all the people who tried to pass by.

"Leave the squirrel alone, Sarah Jessica Barker."

I chuckled at hearing her call Sarah by her full name as if Sarah would listen better now. She would have gotten along with Murphy so well.

"Pria, tell me right now what's going on!"

"She... Sarah's trying to chase a squirrel. I don't know, but she's about to drag us all down with her."

"Listen to me, Pria. Do not let go of the leash no matter what she does. You can't let go."

"I'm trying, but..." Pria screamed. It sounded as if her phone was dragged across the ground and then dropped.

"Pria. Pria, what happened? Answer me. Hello? Hello?" I drew out my hello in the hopes she would hear how worried I was but heard nothing. I looked down at my phone and the call had been dropped.

9

PRIA

GRITTING MY TEETH, I KEPT MY HOLD ON THE LEASHES as I got to my knees and stood up as Sarah tried to pull my arm out of its socket. I was doubtful she and Orvy were brother and sister. She had to have been switched at birth. She was still trying to get that damn squirrel she saw earlier. Was this the way she always reacted when she saw a squirrel because if that was the case, she was never leaving the apartment with me. Maybe I'd hire a dog walker just for her. It would be worth the money. I was lucky Orvy and Jimmy were sitting by my side rather than joining her; I'd be halfway across the state by now.

I could hear my phone's ringtone going off in the distance. I had no idea where I dropped it when I fell and was dragged a few feet down the sidewalk. I was sure to have a huge bruise on my hip. I tried to stop the tears that had started to trail down my cheeks and tamp down my fears of being in charge of these dogs for the next week before taking them back to Kingston's apartment. Swiping my face with the sleeve of my hoodie, I took a deep breath and prepared for battle.

"Sarah," I called firmly as I pulled on her leash. She stopped fighting me but continued to bark incessantly. I held Jimmy and Orvy's leashes in my left hand and Sarah's in my right. I switched so I could hold hers in both hands. I needed all the strength I could get to hold her back from trying to cross the street and chase after that damn squirrel. Luckily, my dead weight had eventually stopped her, otherwise, I would have been sprawled out in the street and probably hit by a car.

My phone started ringing again. Tugging on the leashes, I turned in an attempt to start looking for my phone. It obviously wasn't broken or it wouldn't be ringing which was a plus. All three dogs had their noses to the ground sniffing. I only hoped it wasn't to find any other rodents to chase. They seemed amenable to following behind me as I tracked my phone with Beyoncé belting out the lyrics to "Single Ladies." I'd changed it from "Time After Time" right before I got in the elevator the other night and broke down. Kingston finding me had not been in my plans. I thought I'd been alone and free to finally let loose the tears I'd been holding back all day. I was wrong. Just like I was wrong about so many things in my life. Haider was my biggest mistake. I'd lost years of my life to him only to find out I'd been replaceable with a leggy redhead. My phone had been silent since I'd changed my ringtone except when Kingston called me earlier and now it only reminded me how I was now single and probably always would be. Although, right now, I was fine with that. I didn't need a man in my life to be successful. I only needed myself.

The ringing stopped and my heart dropped. I was never going to be able to find my phone. It could be anywhere. Under a car, in the bushes, or hidden behind a bike tire. Then as if God was listening, the ringing started back up again. I'm not sure how I saw my screen light up with the bright sun shining down making it nearly impossible, but I saw it between a trash can and a newspaper stand. Dragging the dogs behind me, I fought to reach my phone before whoever it was that was calling hung up or the dogs started to drag me in another direction. Picking it up, I fought against the taut leashes to answer.

"Hello?" I hated the sound of my voice wavering, but I couldn't hide the toll the dogs had taken on me. Well, not all the dogs just Sarah. She was now my nemesis. No treats for her this afternoon.

"Pria?" A deep baritone rang with worry. I pulled my phone away and looked down at the number again. It was one I didn't recognize. "Pria, are you there?"

"Kingston? Is that you?" Who else sounded like Kingston Avery with that deep voice that usually sounded so cocky? No one, but why would he be worried about me? Maybe he was worried about the dogs. That had to be it.

"For fuck's sake, Pria, who else would it be? We talked only a few minutes ago. How is it you didn't recognize my voice or my number?"

"No one," I sighed dejectedly. Tears stung the backs of my eyes at my realization. "I'm sorry, I didn't recognize you. Things were a little crazy. Can I call you when I get back to your apartment?" There was no way I was going to be able to talk on the phone and walk the dogs back. And try not to cry because there was no way in hell he was going to see or hear me cry again.

"Are you okay?" The worry in his voice did funny things to me that I wasn't sure if I liked.

"I don't know. Nothing's broken. At least I don't think there is, but you put me in charge of a demon dog and she'll probably kill me if I try to walk and talk at the same time."

"Pria, I'm—" I cut him off. I could hear the apology in his voice, and it was the last thing I needed in that moment. I would have broken down and never would have made it back the half mile to his apartment. Either that or Sarah would have sensed my weakness and killed us all by pulling us into the street.

"Don't. Please." My chin quivered, and I hoped it was impossible to hear my weakness through the phone. "I'll call you back once I get back and things are settled down. Is this the number I can reach you at?"

There was a long pause. I wasn't sure if it was because he wanted to argue with me or if it was because he could hear the defeat in my voice. "This is my cell phone. You can reach me on it day or night." He paused again. "Call me back." That time it was a demand. I wasn't sure if it was the command of him being my boss or if it was his personality. Either way, I'd call him. Eventually.

My right hip throbbed with each step I took making the trek back to the apartment slow going. Sarah had calmed down and was following beside me dutifully. Jimmy Chew kept looking up at me with his sweet little eyes. I wasn't sure if he was checking to see if I was okay or if he wanted me to hold him. Even though he probably only weighed five pounds, I couldn't hold him. There was no way I was going to keep myself vulnerable for Sarah to strike again.

What took us five minutes to walk before took close to forty-five minutes on the way back, I was walking so slow with my now bum hip. I was proud that I kept the situation under control and didn't cry as I walked back with a huge hole in my leggings. I still got looks from all the people who passed me, but I didn't care; I wouldn't see them again after this week.

Stepping inside the apartment, I let out a sigh of relief. We made it. I dropped the leashes and headed into the kitchen for a bottle of water and to give the two male dogs treats. They'd been wonderful. It was almost as if they knew I'd been hurt and tried to take it easy on me. Sarah lifted her snout up in the air and walked out of the room. I didn't care. She could be pissed all she wanted. I had the scrapes and bruises to show for why I wasn't her biggest fan.

After giving Jimmy and Orvy an extra treat, I headed to my room to take a shower. I had dirt all over me and I was hoping it would help me feel better like when you're sick. It seemed to take half an hour to remove my clothes without causing too much pain. If I didn't have a scrape on some part of me, I had a bruise. I guess it was good that I was working from the apartment until Kingston got back. I didn't want everyone at work to see me looking like I'd gotten into a fight. After all the adrenaline left me, I'd be feeling every little bump and scratch. Maybe once I got out of the shower, I'd start drinking the bottle of wine Kingston had in the fridge. It couldn't hurt.

Relaxing back on the couch with a dog on each side and an almost empty wineglass in hand, my phone started to ring from the other room. Shit. I'd forgotten to call Kingston back, and I was sure he was unhappy with me.

I felt very little pain as I got up, thanks to the almost empty bottle of wine, in search of my phone. Had I left it in the kitchen or the bedroom? With how big his apartment was I deduced it was in the kitchen since I wouldn't be able to hear it if I'd left it all the way back in the guest room. Both Orvy and Jimmy followed me into the kitchen. Their tails wagged happily the entire way. They were probably hoping for more treats. I'd give them all the treats in the house for being so sweet to me. I hadn't seen Sarah since she lifted her nose at me and walked away and that was fine by me. If I had to see her, I'd only think about the next time I had to walk her later today and that almost gave me a panic attack.

The same number lit my screen as before when Kingston called me. Once I got off the phone with him, I'd add him to my contact list. I hated not seeing the name of whoever was calling me. Just like I hated having any notifications whatsoever on my phone.

"I'm so sorry. I forgot to call you back," I rushed out. I headed to the pantry to get my new friends their treats as I waited for my boss to go off on me. My phone was quiet for so long, I had to pull it away to make sure the call hadn't been disconnected. Had he hung up on me? One look told me he was still on the line, so either he had a bad connection or was speechless. I was going to go with him having a bad connection. "Hello? Kingston?"

"I'm here," he cleared his throat. "You apologized, and it shocked me."

I wasn't the hard-ass out of the two of us. I had no problem apologizing when I knew I'd done wrong.

"I'm sorry if you were worried about the dogs. I should have called you once we got back to give you an update. They're doing fine. Jimmy and Orvy are so sweet and I've got two new friends."

Again, he was quiet for so long I had to look down at my phone. What the hell was going on with him? Maybe he was sick or jet lagged from his flight. That had to have been it. Or a bad connection.

"I wasn't worried about the dogs, Pria. I know how big and strong Sarah and Orville are. Fuck," he cursed. "I should have thought about you taking care of them. You're not trained with dogs and they're a handful when out to say the least. If anyone should be apologizing it should be me."

Had hell frozen over? Kingston Avery had apologized to me. I turned to the window to see if pigs were flying by.

"Are you feeling okay?" I asked when I didn't see either pigs flying or the world outside turned into the Arctic.

"Tired. Jet lagged, but beside that I'm fine. After I ate dinner and hadn't heard back from you, I decided I should check on you to make sure you're okay."

Oh, that was nice of him. Nice and uncharacteristic. *Do you really know him? You haven't seen him in at least ten years, and he was a sweet boy growing up.* And that reminded me that I still hadn't told him I knew him and his family when we were younger.

"I'm fine and dandy." I grabbed the wine bottle and took it back into the sitting room that overlooked the city. The view was gorgeous and mesmerizing. Sitting down, I poured the small amount that was left of the bottle into my glass and took a sip from it. It was probably the best wine I'd ever had in my life and since it was in Kingston Avery's refrigerator, I was sure it was expensive.

"Are you drunk?" I smiled at how light his tone had turned.

"I'm not sure I'd call me drunk, but I would say buzzed." Jimmy looked up at me sweetly from the floor. I picked him up and put him on my lap. Once Orvy saw Jimmy by me, he stepped easily onto the couch and snuggled up to my side. This was why Kingston had all those crazy rules about them. They were the sweetest things alive. I was going to miss them when I had to leave. "I drank the bottle of wine that you had in your fridge." Shit. "I hope you weren't saving it for something special."

"No, I had it in my refrigerator for my dog walker."

Okay, now I knew he was fucking with me.

"I'll get you a new bottle before you're back so you can drink it with your girlfriend." Even if it did cost me a paycheck.

"Pria," he drew my name out with irritation, "I don't care about the wine. You can drink all the wine in my place if you want. Although, that's a lot of wine to drink in only one week." He ended on a low chuckle.

That got my attention. "Where's the rest of the wine?" I was feeling like another bottle tonight.

"If you can find it, you can drink it. How's that?"

"Sounds like a challenge. One that I happily accept." I rose from my comfy seat to see if I could find his wine stash. Jimmy wasn't happy I dumped him on the couch.

Turning around with wide eyes, I realized I'd been letting the dogs on the couch since we'd been back from their walk and they weren't supposed to be on any of the furniture. I couldn't ask them to get down while I was on the phone so I let them be. What harm could they do being on the couch for a week?

"You're looking for it right now aren't you?" His low laugh set off butterflies in my stomach. They could fuck right off. I couldn't have butterflies for my boss.

"Maybe," I hummed. "Do you want me to save a bottle for your girlfriend?" There was no secret wine cabinet in the kitchen so I moved to the other end of the apartment I hadn't been in. I figured if it was by my bedroom I would have noticed. My nose could sniff out wine when it was within a two hundred foot radius. Now that I was walking around, my buzz had changed to full on drunk, and all my aches and pains were long gone.

"Why do I get the impression that you're fishing to see if I have a girlfriend?" The amusement in his voice made me sober some, encouraging me to search for another bottle even more.

"Does she not like wine? Good, all the more for me."

"Why were you drinking?" he asked quietly, sobering me more. I needed to get off the phone before I was fully sober again. Or before those damn butterflies took flight from his quiet words and concern. It shouldn't take so little for me to swoon, but damn if I was, and it needed to stop.

"Because the she-devil that lives in your house hates me. She nearly killed me today. I'm black and blue with scratches everywhere. I don't know how

I'm going to be able to take her out again. Seriously, just thinking about it is causing me to panic."

Kingston swore on the other end of the line and then I heard typing on his end. What the hell was he doing? "I never should have asked you to watch them. I wanted to help you out and now I've made the situation worse. Let me see if I can figure something out with Sarah. She can be a handful."

A handful? She was so far beyond a handful, but I wasn't going to argue. If he could take Sarah off my hands, I would be fine. If he found someone to deal with her, would I have to leave? Surely they'd be able to handle all three. Unlike me.

"Will I have to leave?" The minute the words left my mouth I wanted to take them back. Why was I giving him the thought?

"Do you want to leave?"

"No," I answered honestly. "I hate that I'm causing you more problems. Why can't your dogs learn how to use the toilet? That would make this so much easier."

A booming laugh came from Kingston. It could melt panties even over the phone. "You really are drunk. It does sound nice though. It would make my life easier." He yawned, making me look for the time. It had to be getting late there, and I was keeping him up by making him worry about me and his dogs.

"Tonight I'll take Sarah by herself before I take the

other two. I think if it's one on one, I'll be able to handle her better." If not, he was going to find a lot of puppy puddles on his floor when he got back. "We'll be fine. Don't worry about us. You should get some rest for your meeting tomorrow."

"Are you sure? I don't want you to get hurt again." The last word was drawn out by a long yawn.

"I'm positive. I'll show her who's boss." I wasn't positive, and I was sure she'd put up a fuss if she didn't get her way. I was seeing her diva ways. How was she related to Orville, I didn't know.

"You do that and if you need anything, you've got my contact info." He sounded lighter, and I was happy to know I had relaxed him some. He probably thought I was some incompetent fool. He'd probably come home from London and fire me, leaving me without a job and homeless.

"I do, but I promise you won't hear from me again. I've got this."

Sarah stood at the door of what I assumed was Kingston's room as if on guard. I turned around and went to look for more wine elsewhere.

I so didn't have this.

10

PRIA

COVERING MY HEAD WITH MY PILLOW, I TRIED TO FALL asleep while one of the dogs howled. It had been going on for the last hour and I didn't see it ending anytime soon. It was rounding on midnight and I was now one hundred percent sober. Maybe if I had found the wine, I would have been asleep and oblivious to the crying of whoever was out there.

Throwing the pillow across the room, I got out of bed and made my way out to where Orville stood in the middle of the living room, howling at the top of his lungs. Or at least it seemed like it because it was loud as fuck. I was sure if Kingston's apartment didn't span the entire top floor, someone would be calling the police because this was a disturbance of epic proportions in the middle of the night. I knew I would have called the police if I could.

Folding down in front of him to sit on the floor, I

ran my hand down Orvy's back. "What's going on, buddy? Did you get hurt today?" He'd seemed fine, but it would be my luck that he was injured and would need medical attention. I ran my hands over his whole body but found nothing. I was surprised it quieted him down. "You're okay, big guy. Go to sleep and I'll see you in the morning."

Pulling to stand, I dragged myself back to my bed and gently climbed in. Drinking hadn't been the best idea. I was tired from the wine and needed sleep. Plus, now I could feel all the sore places. Every inch of my entire body.

I had started to drift off to sleep when another howl broke me from my tired haze. Heaven help me, what did Orville want? Again, I climbed out of bed and found Orvy where I'd left him. I scratched behind his ears and he seemed to like my attention. After a few moments, I stopped and went back to bed. This cycle continued for the next thirty minutes. I was tired and annoyed. All I wanted was to sleep, but it seemed that wasn't going to happen unless it was on the floor in the living room. I knew it was extremely early in London, but I didn't know what else to do except call Kingston. Yes, I'd made a promise not to bother him anymore, but I cared more about my sleep in that moment than anything else. This time when I went to make Orvy stop crying, I brought my phone with me. I had no idea what was wrong with him, but his sad cries were killing me so I called his owner.

Kingston answered on the fourth ring. "Hello?" he answered groggily. "Pria? Can this wait? It's a little after five here."

"I know and I'm sorry to be calling so early, but I didn't know what else to do. Orvy won't stop crying unless I come out to the living room and pet him. Once I go back to my room, he cries until I come back out. We've been on repeat for the last hour and all I want to do is sleep." I knew I sounded whiny, but I didn't care. I wanted sleep, and I'd do anything to get it.

Kingston groaned and even though I was dead tired, it sent tingles through my entire body. How could he sound so sexy this early in the morning?

"From the day I brought Orvy home, he's always been a crier at night. I thought it was just me and he'd be fine." I rolled my eyes. Of course, he thought the dog only cried for him. Kingston was that self-centered. "After half a night of him crying, I gave in and let him sleep with me. Just let him sleep in bed with you and he'll be fine."

I had to have heard him wrong. There was no way he said to let that horse of a dog in my bed. It may have been a king-size, but he'd take up more of it than me. When I slept, I was all over the bed and I didn't want to battle for space with Orvy. Haider hated it. He complained frequently that I'd smack him in the face or elbow him multiple times a night if he didn't snuggle with me, and he hated snuggling.

Sucked to be Haider.

"There's nothing else I can do? Maybe he'll be happy to just sleep in your bed." It could be the bed he wanted and not the man. The bed in the guest room was the most comfortable bed I'd ever slept on and if that was the bed Kingston put in the guest bedroom then I couldn't imagine what he'd put in his own bedroom.

"You can try, but I don't think it will do you any good. He loves being around people day and night. Now, why don't you try that, so I get another hour of sleep." I still wasn't sure if he was telling me the truth or not. He could say anything to get off the phone with me, but he had to know that I would call him back no matter the time if Orville continued crying.

"Fine. You better be right," I snapped. "If not, I'm calling you back so you don't get any sleep either."

"I wouldn't expect anything less, but you'll see, Orvy just wants to cuddle with you. Good night, Pria." He hung up without me replying.

I eyed Orville and his large body. This was going to be interesting. Maybe he wouldn't like sleeping with me and he'd leave. Anything was possible.

"Come on, Orvy. Let's go to bed." His big ears

perked up, and I knew then he'd be in my bed all night and for the rest of the week. I felt bad about leaving Jimmy out in the living room, but he seemed content in his plush little bed. I hadn't seen Sarah after we came back from her solo walk and that was fine by me. She was probably back in Kingston's room guarding his wine.

I guess it could be worse. I could have a hangover from the bottle I drank earlier. A hangover along with a stiff and aching body would be hell, so I was thankful, or I would be after I got some sleep.

Orvy and I padded down the hall to my bedroom and it was like he knew exactly what was going on. The second we stepped foot into the room, he went straight to the bed, jumped up, and started to make himself comfortable in the middle. I was slower getting into bed, thanks to his sister. I moved like an old lady trying to get comfortable. I faced out because even though I like the big mutt; I didn't want to have his dog breath in my face as I tried to sleep.

Shit. I forgot to brush their teeth. Oh well, one night wouldn't kill them. On a scale of one to ten, I was at a negative two on following the rules. And I still wasn't sure if all of them were real or not. How did you brush a dog's teeth without them biting you? Tomorrow, I was going to be watching all the YouTube videos I could find on taking care of dogs.

Closing my eyes, I snuggled deep into ultra-soft

sheets until I felt Orvy stand. Looking over my shoulder my eyes slowly adjusted to the dark room to find him standing in the middle of the bed looking at me. Okay, creeper. I couldn't sleep knowing he was staring down at me.

"What is it, Orvy?" I groaned. "It's time to sleep. Please." Turning over until I was on my back, I patted the bed by my hip. Of course, he took that as an invitation to lay with his body molded to mine. I guess Orville really was a cuddler. His warm body against mine soothed some of the ache out of my muscles making it easy to fall asleep with him next to me.

Who knew dogs could be sleep aids?

11

KINGSTON

MY PHONE VIBRATED IN MY POCKET. I DIDN'T CARE WHO it was if I could take a break from the meeting from hell. We couldn't agree on anything. I'd listened to why it was a good idea for me to buy out their company and how they would change things so I didn't lose all the money from buying them out. It didn't seem possible. I'd need to speak to Whitmore when I got back and see why he thought we could make this our London office. Although I wanted to expand my company, I wasn't sure I was ready to take it internationally. I didn't want to travel out of the country all the time, so if—and that was a big if— I bought out Harper Capital, I'd need to find someone else to run it. Which meant more work for me.

"Excuse me." I stood holding my phone so they could see I needed to take this phone call. I hit the green icon and answered. "Give me a minute." I hadn't even looked to see who it was I was so happy for the interruption. Now that I was heading down the hallway, I looked down to see it was Pria. "I thought you weren't going to call—"

"Oh my God, Kingston. I think I've poisoned Jimmy and my calls to the vet aren't going through."

"What the fuck, Pria? You're not supposed to kill my dogs while I'm gone." Everyone on the floor was looking at me, but I didn't care. Pria was going to be the end of me and my dogs. "What happened?" I growled out, my teeth grinding together.

"I don't know. I swear I'm not trying to kill your dogs. I love Jimmy and Orvy." Her voice cracked and I swear my heart stopped beating for a second. "Everything was going great. I took the dogs out this morning. Sarah by herself and she seems to enjoy it only being her and then the boys. After we came back, we all ate our breakfasts, and I started to work. I set my laptop on the dining room table. I—"

"I don't give a fuck where you set up shop. I want to know what's happening with my dog and why you think you poisoned him. Are you sure you didn't get the vet's number wrong in your frazzled state?"

I was going to murder her if Jimmy died while I was away. He was the first dog my sister had rescued and given to me. He was the best dog and I couldn't lose him. Not now or ever.

"It's possible. I'm so worried about poor Jimmy. He was lying in his bed and made this sad sound. I went to check him and his stomach is all distended. I don't know what to do or know of another vet. I thought you might know what to do." Her voice shook, but I didn't give a shit if Pria was upset. She was trying to kill Jimmy.

"No, I don't know of another vet off the top of my head; that's why I left you the sheet with all the important numbers on it. Let me see if I can get ahold of the vet. Stay on the line." Before she could answer, I switched lines, pulled the vet's number and called them. They answered on the third ring and I sighed in relief and annoyance. How could she have gotten the phone number wrong? Who knew Pria was so incompetent at dog care? Since I didn't know what was going on I brought Pria on the line to answer their questions.

"I've got one of the vet techs on the line now. They have some questions for you." I tried not to sound as pissed off as I was, but there was no hiding it. I stepped into an unoccupied conference room to have a little privacy and sat down at the table. Closing my eyes, I kept the phone to my ear as I listened.

"What seems to be the problem? Mr. Avery said Jimmy's belly is distended. Are there any other symptoms?"

"Um… I'm not really well versed in dogs. It's only my third day with them. I took him for his morning walk and bathroom break and when we came back, I fed them the leftover stew from last night. It was a small portion and he still seemed hungry so after I ate all my cereal, I let him have the rest of the milk that was in the bowl."

She what? That was not a part of Jimmy nor the others' dietary guidelines.

"And how long afterward did you notice his belly?"

"I'm not sure since I was working. I heard a little noise come from him and I thought I smelled something unpleasant so I went over to check on him. His stomach was easy to see and when I put my hand on it, it felt hard. Was it the leftovers?"

"No, sweetie it wasn't the leftovers. It sounds like Jimmy is lactose intolerant and isn't handling the milk you gave him very well."

"Intolerant?" Pria mumbled. "That doesn't seem right. Don't dogs drink milk from their mothers."

"Yes, they do, but after they're weaned they no longer drink milk, and it's easy for them to become intolerant to something they no longer need in their diet."

"But don't people always set out milk for dogs to drink. Jimmy loved it."

"I'm sure he did, dear. He probably liked the

sugariness of it, but he's not loving it now. From now on let's make sure not to give him any more milk. The milk people leave out for pets or strays isn't for dogs, but for kittens."

"That's stupid. Dogs should be able to have milk too. Why are people only leaving stuff out for cats?" Her argument and irritation caused my lips to twitch, but I'd never let her know it.

"I'm not sure why, but if Jimmy doesn't get better in a few hours or gets worse please, bring him into the clinic and we'll look him over."

"I can't bring him in now and you'll make him feel better?" She sounded like she was about to cry. It was obvious that Pria had become attached to Jimmy.

"I wish there was something we could do, but there's no fix to lactose intolerance except to wait it out. Do you have any more questions or concerns before we get off the line?"

I let out a sigh of relief to know that Jimmy was okay, and it was likely just built up gas that was causing his stomach to distend. I wanted to rail on Pria for not following the rules, but I didn't want to upset her more and cause her to leave. Since I no longer trusted the people the agency sent, I wasn't sure who I could get to watch the dogs from now on when I traveled or had to work late. I had already put in some calls but hadn't heard anything back yet.

Murphy would have watched them. She loved

them and spending time with them. My chest hurt thinking of my sister and how I'd never see her again.

"Not right now," Pria answered sounding unsure. "Can I call you with any questions?"

"Yes, dear. We also have an overnight call center that can answer any of your questions. If that's all, I suggest you try to make Jimmy as comfortable as possible until this passes."

"I will. Thank you and thank you for being so nice."

Nice? Did she want me to be nice when she called me saying she'd poisoned my dog and that he might be dying? No one was going to handle that news lightly.

"You're welcome, dear."

There was a pause of silence. Neither Pria nor I said a word. Maybe she thought I'd hung up after the vet tech got on the line. If she thought I would hang up without knowing what was wrong with my dog, she was in for a rude surprise.

"Are you still there?" She broke the silence.

"I'm still here." I didn't bother hiding my irritation at her incompetence.

"I didn't know, Kingston. I'm really sorry I bothered you and probably took you away from an important meeting. I'm failing at something that should be so simple." She sniffed, and I'd never been happier to be across the pond. I knew I'd forgive her in an instant if I saw her with tears in her eyes.

I knew taking care of my trio of dogs wasn't easy, and if I were a nice guy, I wouldn't take out my frustrations on her, but I couldn't help it. "Just try not to fuck up again," I growled and disconnected the call.

Gritting my teeth, I pushed from the conference table and headed out of the room. I was done for the day. I didn't care what else Ms. Sinclair had planned; I was leaving with or without her blessing. Not that I cared what she thought of me. They'd be lucky if I bought them out.

Hitting the down button on the elevator, I tapped my foot as I waited. I was going to head back to my hotel room, open the minibar and start drinking. I didn't plan to stop until after dinner and every bottle was empty.

"Mr. Avery, where are you going?" I heard the clack of Ms. Sinclair's heels before I saw her. As the doors opened, her eyes widened and her feet picked up speed.

"I've got all the information I need to make an informed decision. I'll have Whitmore let you know what we decide." I hit the button for the ground floor and pulled out my phone. I'd need for my new secretary, whatever her name was, to change my flight.

"But we weren't done."

"We're done." I needed to head home first thing in the morning.

The "O" shape of her mouth turned into a thin line as the doors slowly closed. I wasn't sure if she was disappointed my trip was coming to an end early because of the likelihood she wouldn't get a chance to sleep with me or if it was because she knew the chance of Avery Capital Holdings taking over was slim to none.

Either way, I didn't care. I was finished with London.

12

PRIA

I WAS ATTEMPTING THE UNTHINKABLE. I WAS WALKING all three dogs at one time and taking them to the dog park. It was a beautiful fall day, and I wanted to spend it outside enjoying the sunshine. I could have left Sarah back at the apartment, but I didn't think that would be fair. Luckily, no squirrel had crossed our path.

I'd spent a good part of the morning researching dog parks in the area. They all seemed to be good, so I went with the one closest to Kingston's apartment. It was still far enough away to cause me anxiety with all the dogs. Sarah was constantly pulling ahead and tugging me along while Orvy and Jimmy stayed by my side. It was like that in the apartment too. The only time I saw Sarah was when I was feeding them. She didn't come out when it was time to brush their teeth and I was thankful for that. I had a feeling she would have bitten me if I tried to push the issue. Surprisingly, it wasn't all that hard, but I had a feeling it was because they were used to it. It helped that I watched a few videos on how to do it. I couldn't imagine what would have happened if I hadn't. Even the sweet Jimmy might have bitten me if I had pried his mouth open and started brushing his teeth the way I'd imagined doing it.

After thirty minutes of me biting my bottom lip to the point it bled because of nerves, we made it to the dog park. They each sat patiently as I unclipped their leashes before they ran off one by one. I wasn't sure how I was going to get them back on them now that they were out in the wild, but I'd tackle that problem once I was ready to leave.

I found a bench and pulled out a book I'd been wanting to read but never had time until now. I couldn't remember the last time I'd read a book, which was sad. I loved to read, but Haider had always complained about me needing the light on at night so I could read when he wanted to go to sleep. He really was a douche. Why had I let him change so much about me? Why had I settled for substandard sex? Especially with a man who had tried to stifle me almost from the get-go.

I made a promise to myself in that moment that I'd never let another man hold me back. Nor would I continue to have sex with any man who sucked in bed. Whenever I finally had sex again, since I didn't see it in my near future.

At the beginning of every chapter, I would peak up and find each dog. Sarah and Orvy weren't hard to find since they were so large, but Jimmy was another matter. After finishing the fifth chapter, I quickly found Sarah laying down on the grass, her head held high and a few dogs sniffing around her. She looked regal and like a true diva. Orvy was running with another dog, his tongue sticking out. If he could, he'd be smiling. Coming to the park had been a great decision.

I scanned the park in search of Jimmy but didn't see him. I had to do a double take when I swore I saw a goat standing amongst the dogs. I couldn't remember ever seeing or mistaking a dog for a goat or vice versa so I put my book away and headed in the direction of what couldn't possibly be a dog because it was an honest to goodness goat.

In all my research about the dog parks, I didn't see anything about being able to bring other animals. The goat wasn't bothering anyone or the dogs, but it was still strange. As I walked up to said goat, Jimmy came out of nowhere and started to hump one of its legs. After he'd been attached to my leg all morning as I looked up information, I couldn't imagine he'd have the energy or the need to hump anything else for some time, but I was wrong. Jimmy obviously wasn't picky about who he tried to get it on with. His theme song should be "Let's Get It On" by Marvin Gaye.

The goat fainted as Jimmy tried to procreate and make little *doat* babies. My feet moved faster than they'd ever moved before as I sprinted toward the now dead goat. I was going to feel this later, but I didn't care. I dropped down to my knees and cradled the head of the goat in my hands.

"Please wake up. Please. Oh my God, I'm the worst dog sitter on the planet. Can one day go by without something horrible happening? Come on, goat. Please don't be dead," I cried. Jimmy came to stand on the side of my leg and looked down at the goat he tried to make babies with and instead gave it a heart attack. "Jimmy, why do you have to hump everything? I thought we had something special. If I would have known you were going to sex up the park, I would have left you at home."

A soft feminine laugh came from beside me. "She's not dead. Trust me."

"Are you the goat whisperer or something? Did you see her drop from Jimmy humping her?"

"I did see, that's why I was on my way over here. Then I saw you making a beeline for them and stayed out of the way. You were on a mission and I didn't want to get in the way. I thought you might plow right over me." She laughed, giving me levity to the situation. I hoped she knew what she was talking about.

"I probably wouldn't have been able to stop, so good call. Do you really think she's okay?" I asked, hopeful. I couldn't live with myself if I was responsible for this goat's death.

"She's perfectly fine. Look at her chest. It's going up and down." It was indeed rising and falling. Now I felt stupid. "She faints when she's scared and she scares easily. I doubt she was expecting to feel a little dog going to town on her leg." I looked to see a woman with long auburn hair and wide green eyes smile down at me.

"Neither was I the first time I met him."

"Did you faint?"

"No, the goat has that on me. Is this goat yours?"

"She is." She knelt next to me and ran a hand down the side of the goat. "I'm Aubrey, by the way, and this is Pixy."

"I'm Pria and this little guy is Jimmy Chew."

"Cute name." She smiled and scratched behind Jimmy's ears. If she wasn't careful, he'd be humping her leg next.

"I agree, but I didn't name him. It's my boss's dog. There are two more running around here somewhere."

"Wow, you're brave bringing three dogs. You must be a natural with animals."

I couldn't help but laugh. "I'm the furthest thing from a natural. I can't seem to do anything right when it comes to these dogs."

"Well, you're obviously caring and that's all that matters." She pointed to Pixy and her eyes fluttered open. One second she was out and the next she hopped up and walked away before running into a tree.

"Are you sure she's okay?"

"Oh yeah, aside from fainting at the drop of a hat, she's also blind."

"Wow, there must never be a dull moment with her around." Picking up Jimmy, I slowly stood.

"Pixy and my husband definitely make for an interesting and fun life."

"I didn't know dog parks allowed other animals," I blurted out. "I'm sorry. It's none of my business. I'm just surprised."

"Don't be." She giggled. "I used to be a lawyer, so I threatened to sue if they didn't allow us in. Their rules don't state no other animals to be allowed in the park. Plus, we donate a lot of money to the park and the rescue shelter in the area."

"Money makes the world go round," I mumbled.

"Sadly, it does. Pixy is my baby and I don't see why just because she's a goat she should be excluded. My husband thinks I'm crazy, but he puts up with it and often has to do the dirty work. We're here in town to try and give all animals equal rights."

I arched my brow at that. I wasn't sure how they were going to do that. I understood a goat, but I wouldn't want some animal that could eat my pet at the same park. "All animals?"

"Well, not *all* obviously. We can't have alligators here, but why not sweet farm animals? Why can't someone who has a pet pig bring them to an animal park?"

She did make a point. I'd like to see a cute little piggy wandering around. "Farm animals make sense. Maybe you could start your own park that welcomes all animals or farm animals."

Aubrey's eyes lit up. "You get it! Yes, that's what we're trying to do here and the one by our house in California. We recently raised enough money for the one in California and after news spread the shelter that's here about a block away contacted us about doing a fundraiser to raise awareness and try to get the rules changed here."

"Good luck." I wasn't sure how well that would work, and I was pretty sure goats were forbidden in New York. Maybe they'd gotten special permission. Come to think of it, there were quite a few animals that were forbidden from being pets in the city.

"So, you're watching your boss's dogs? Is that normal?" The twinkle in her green eyes told me she thought something more was going on between Kingston and me.

Placing Jimmy back on the ground to probably hump another dog or ten, I told her about how I'd come to work for Kingston Avery, finding my boyfriend cheating on me, why I didn't want to stay at my dad's house, and finally the offer to take care of Kingston's dogs while he was out of town. I didn't usually open up to people that easily, but there was something about Aubrey that made her easy to talk to.

"Sounds like a nice guy. Are you sure watching his dogs is all that's going on between you two?"

I wanted to laugh in her face, but that would have been rude. Plus, she seemed really nice. "Nothing's going on. He may be gorgeous, but he's my boss, and that means nothing can happen between us."

Her smile grew. "Just because he's your boss doesn't mean nothing can happen. Especially if he's gorgeous."

"It's against company policy. I should know; I'm the director of HR."

Aubrey wiggled her eyebrows but said no more on the subject. "Obviously your boss loves animals since he has three dogs. Do you think if I gave you some information he might donate or be a sponsor for Paws and Claws?"

I didn't know the company or Kingston well

enough to answer that. "You can send me the information and I'll make sure he gets it. I can't promise anything though. I've only been with the company for a short time."

"That would be great. Would you like to attend the fundraiser? Maybe go with your boss?"

This time I didn't hold back my laugh. "I told you there's nothing there, but I'll definitely come. Maybe I can meet a handsome and generous man who loves animals while I'm there."

"I have a feeling you don't have to look too far to find the man you're looking for." Aubrey's phone buzzed, stopping her from saying anything more. "Shoot. It looks like I need to go. Give me your information real quick and I'll send you something in the next few days." Rattling off my email address, I looked around for the dogs. It was probably time to start heading back to the apartment. I still needed to put their dinner in the crockpot. Hell, their dinners smelled so good I was tempted to eat along with them. No one would know if I did.

"It was good meeting you, Pria. I hope to see you at the fundraiser." Aubrey waved as she headed toward Pixy.

"It was good meeting you too."

EVERYTHING WAS GOING SO WELL. THE DOGS SEEMED TO have gotten all their energy out at the park. No one was tugging on their leash as we headed back to the apartment. By no one, I meant Sarah. She seemed to be in a good mood, and I was going to treat her for it once we got upstairs.

I knew I shouldn't have been counting my lucky stars. One minute everything was great and the next, first one squirrel and then another ran right in front of us. If any animal should have been banned from New York, it should have been squirrels; they were trouble with a capital *T*. Sarah darted for one and then the other nearly ripping my arm off. The girl was seriously strong.

Instead of letting her take me down like she did the first day, I let go of the leash. At the time it seemed like the right thing to do until I watched Sarah run like her ass was on fire down the sidewalk after the squirrels. Orvy started barking like he was telling her to come back, but she wasn't listening to either one of us.

Scooping Jimmy into my arms, I took off after Sarah. It really was like trying to run after a horse. One second she was there and the next she was gone. Completely out of sight. One block and then another, I tried to catch up to her as I screamed her name over and over again. My voice was becoming hoarse from yelling. In the distance, I could see her smelling a bush. I yelled Sarah's name again and what did she do? She looked at me, ran toward me only to run right past me. I tried to stomp on her leash as she flew by to no avail.

A runner I was not, and I was starting to slow down. I was surprised I'd lasted as long as I had. When I saw the building Kingston lived in up ahead, I knew I needed to drop the dogs off and head back out as quickly as possible. I couldn't believe this was happening to me. Kingston was going to kill me when he found out I'd lost his dog.

Tears sprung to my eyes as I opened the door. Spotting the doorman, I rushed over dragging Orvy with me. He seemed to want to follow after Sarah and wasn't liking that we'd gone inside. "I don't mean to bother you, but do you by any chance have a key to get to Mr. Avery's penthouse?"

His eyes flicked up and then back down at the paper that was in front of him. "And what would your name be?"

I understood he was doing his job, but I needed to get back out there and look for Sarah. I gripped Orvy's leash tighter and hugged Jimmy to me as I tried to rein in what I wanted to say so this man would take them. Unfortunately, in my time here, I hadn't met this doorman and he didn't know who I was. I understood he was trying to protect the occupants of the building by not letting random people up, but time was of the essence.

"My name is Pria Wang. I'm staying in Kingston Avery's penthouse while he's out of town. I wanted—"

"Yes, I have you down here as his guest. What may I help you with?" He eyed me up and down. I was sure I looked a mess and my voice sounded like I'd smoked twenty packs of cigarettes a day, but I didn't care. I needed his help.

Holding the leashes out to him, I already had one foot aimed at the door ready to leave as soon as I handed them over. "I need you to take Orville and Jimmy up to Mr. Avery's apartment."

He looked down at the dogs, the leashes I was holding out, and then to me. "Where's Sarah?"

Good question.

"She ran away and I need to go find her. Hence why I'm standing here trying to hand over these two. Can. You. Take. Them. Or. Not?" If I had to, I'd take them with me, but it would be easier if I didn't have to worry about them. I had to find Sarah, and the longer I was in here trying to get this bozo to take the other two dogs, the faster my chances of finding her diminished.

His eyes widened and he gasped as if I'd committed a cardinal sin. Or maybe he knew precisely how Kingston would react when he found out the news. Either way, I knew it was bad, but I couldn't help but drop the leash out of instinct when she went chasing after those damn squirrels. Squirrels needed to be banned from this part of town because every time I saw one, I nearly had a panic attack. I was starting to believe I had PTSD from our first walk. I was likely going to have it now after losing her and having to explain all this to Kingston.

"Please take them upstairs so I can continue looking. I need to find her," I begged, thrusting the leashes into his waiting hand before he agreed. "Thanks," I called over my shoulder as I jogged outside.

I didn't get far though. I ran straight into a hard chest. When I looked up, up, and up some more, my gaze was met by the icy green orbs of Kingston Avery.

I was well and truly fucked now.

13

KINGSTON

STEPPING OUT OF MY CAR, I HAD ONLY TAKEN TWO STEPS before Pria ran straight into me. She looked at me in shock and then tears filled her eyes.

Did she know tears were my weakness? I had planned to yell at her when I saw her, and she likely knew. They didn't look fake, especially as one slipped down her cheek and a flood of them followed.

"You're going to hate me." Her lower lip quivered as tears slipped past her perfect pout. "I lost Sarah." My hands tightened on her arms and her head started shaking as she continued to speak. "We were almost here when a fucking squirrel ran out in front of her. Don't they know to stay hidden when she's around?" She didn't let me answer and even if she had, I wouldn't have known what to say to her statement. Pria seemed a little unhinged. "She was about to drag me down and I let go of her leash. We'd had such a nice day, and I thought we'd turned a corner. I dropped Jimmy and Orvy off with the doorman to take them upstairs while I went back out to look for her."

"Which way did she go?" I asked through gritted teeth. I wasn't sure how I was going to look at her day after day if anything happened to Sarah. Was Pria's job in life to piss me off?

"That way." She pulled out of my grip and pointed to the left. "She's so fast."

That she was, but if we were lucky she'd stop by one of the vendors close by and beg for some food. If not, I'm not sure how we'd find her. There were so many places for her to go and there was always the chance someone might try to steal her. It was doubtful with how big she was, but she was a beautiful dog. Who knew? My mind was all over the place on all the possibilities.

"Let's go." I grabbed her hand and started off in a light jog in the direction Pria had pointed.

Even over the city noise, I could hear Pria behind me sniffling every few minutes. I couldn't look back at her or I'd stop and try to console her when I needed to keep my eyes peeled for a large gray dog.

We stopped by the first street vendor, Pria clutching at my arm. "Have you seen a gray Great Dane go by here in the last..." I turned to look down at Pria and her tears nearly wrecked my already breaking heart.

"Twenty minutes, maybe."

"Twenty fucking minutes," I growled under my breath. Did she not realize what could happen in that amount of time? Sarah could easily get hit by a car. She wasn't used to being off her leash unless she was at the dog park. "Maybe she went to the dog park."

"That's where we were coming from. I know she last went this way. I was only in your building for a minute, maybe two and I kept my focus on the windows in case she turned back around." Her tears had dried. Thank God. Now I could be mad at her again.

The vendor finally spoke. "A big dog came sniffing around here about five minutes ago. Headed that way." He pointed to the east. The same way Pria said she was headed.

"Thanks," Pria and I said at the same time.

We took off at a run, looking around every vendor, bush, and between cars. Everywhere. When we reached the Paws and Hearts rescue shelter, I stopped outside and looked in. I didn't see Sarah, but it wouldn't hurt to ask if they'd seen her.

"Stay here. I'm going to ask if they've seen Sarah." Pria's sad eyes looked at me with dead eyes and I didn't wait for a reply.

Two women stood behind the counter chatting

but when they saw me, they straightened and smiled. "Have you seen a Great Dane come by here? My dog walker let go of her leash and now we can't find her."

"Oh no, you lost your puppy. What does she look like?" She batted her eyelashes at me. Why were women always batting their damn eyes at me? All it did was piss me off.

"Big and gray," I answered back a little gruffer than I needed to. "She's a Great Dane."

Her friend seemed to understand that I was annoyed. Putting her hand on the other woman's arm, she frowned. "No, I'm sorry. If you want to leave your contact information, we'll call you if she's brought in or we see her."

"Her name is Sarah. It's on her tag. If you find here, please call me." I slid a business card out of my pocket and placed it on the counter.

Stepping outside, I found Pria huddled underneath the awning. It had started to rain while I was inside. "If you don't want to get wet you can stay here, but I'm going to continue looking for Sarah."

Pria stepped out from under the awning and into the rain. "I'm coming with you."

We trudged along the sidewalk looking everywhere for Sarah. With each passing minute, I knew our chances of finding her were becoming nil. The temperature had dropped around twenty degrees once it started to rain and our teeth had started chattering about half an hour ago. We'd most likely be sick tomorrow, but the only people who knew I was back in town were my secretary and Pria.

"Maybe we should turn around. She could have turned back around, and we wouldn't even know." Pria hung her head and every word that came out of her mouth sounded like a lie. She didn't think Sarah had doubled back, and she didn't think we'd find her either.

"You can head back, but I'm going to keep going this way for a little longer. I know there's another vendor up here and if they say they haven't seen her then I'll turn around."

"I'll stay with you unless you want to go back." Her lips were turning blue and yet she wanted to stick it out with me.

"You're freezing—"

"So are you and this is my fault." Her hands went to her chest. Pria looked miserable. Not only was she freezing but devastated by losing Sarah. "I'll never be able to forgive myself if something happens to Sarah... even if she does hate me. I can't believe I let go of her leash." A tear slipped down her cheek. "I'm so stupid."

I was the stupid one leaving her to take care of my dogs. If I had been thinking I would have known there was no way for her to walk all three. It was her damn tears that had me thinking illogically. "You're not stupid. Now come on, let's go see if they've spotted her."

Wrapping my fingers around her small freezing hand, I wanted to demand Pria go back to my apartment and warm up, but I knew she'd refuse. Instead, I held her hand tighter and trudged along the sidewalk in the direction of the hot dog vendor that I always had to pull Sarah away from.

To my utter disappointment, Sarah was not sniffing around the hot dog man. "Mr. A," Sid called me over, his big frame dwarfing his food cart. "Are you looking for Sarah?"

Hope bloomed as we raced over. "Have you seen her?" Stepping under his tent, my thighs brushed against the warm metal of his cart as my heart started to pound in my chest.

"I have and I gave her a hot dog." Sid knew I never fed my dogs his food. They were on a strict diet to keep them happy and healthy. "Don't give me that look, she was hungry and alone."

I guessed I couldn't hide my unhappiness at his admission. "How long ago did you see her?"

He see-sawed his head back and forth. "Probably around two minutes ago. I tried to get her to stay with me because I knew you'd be coming to find her. You take such good care of your babies." They weren't my babies. They were Murphy's babies. I had

been their foster parent when she got sick and then...
now they were mine.

"He does," Pria chimed in from beside me. Her small hand grasped my bicep making my body instantly relax. How had she known to do that? Time was wasting and if we didn't find Sarah soon, she'd either be lost or hit by a car. "Which way did Sarah go?"

"Yes, yes." Sid nodded his head rapidly. "You should go find her. She went the way you always come from."

Maybe she was headed home. "Thanks, Sid, for looking out for her." I pulled my business card out of my suit pocket and wrote my cell phone number on it. "If you see her again, please call me."

"Sure thing, Mr. A."

I took off running. How had I let myself become so attached to these dogs? I knew better than anyone to not get attached, because eventually everyone you loved, no matter how much you loved someone, left you.

The moment my building came into view, my stomach dropped. I expected to see a big gray dog standing outside waiting for me. Instead, there was nothing. Not a single soul was around. The slapping of shoes behind me had me turning around to see Pria running toward me with her arms wrapped around herself. Even from feet away, I could tell she was freezing by the way her arms didn't swing and the slight blue tint to her lips. Her almond-shaped eyes darted around the area as she neared.

"No Sarah?" she mouthed.

I started to shake my head, unable to speak the words out loud when I spotted the day doorman, George, squatting down in front of my beautiful dog. Darting inside, I ran over to Sarah and wrapped her in a big hug.

"The young lady staying with you mentioned Sarah was lost, so I was keeping an eye out for her. When I saw her sniffing around outside, I brought her inside. I was about to take her upstairs with the others." George clamored from beside me.

Standing to my full height, I shook his hand. "Thank you for all your help, George." I wanted to say more but didn't want him to think because he found Sarah we'd start talking every time we saw each other. Everyone in the building knew not to talk to me if they saw me in passing or on the elevator.

"You're most welcome, Mr. Avery." His dark eyes twinkled, and I knew I needed to end this now.

"Oh, you found her." Pria's soft voice floated over us and relief was evident in her tone. She knelt down and hugged Sarah for a long moment. If I hadn't known how upset she'd been, I would have laughed as Sarah tried to escape her arms. Pria stood shakily with her arms once again wrapped around herself.

Even though it was warm inside, she still must have been freezing.

"Why don't we head up and get you warm?" Taking Sarah's leash, I ushered Pria toward the elevator with her shuffling along behind me.

"Kingston, I'm so sorry," Pria muttered from beside me as the elevator doors slowly closed. "Please don't fire me."

Gritting my teeth, I tried to keep my tone calm. Being an asshole right now wouldn't do me any favors. "Do you think so little of me?" I didn't want to think about how if something had happened to Sarah or Orvy and Jimmy, I likely would have found some way to fire her without being sued.

"Well, I... um... I..." she stuttered and looked around nervously.

"Obviously you do, or you wouldn't have said that." I tightened my hold on the leash as I turned toward her. Her lips were still slightly blue, and I knew it was because she'd been out for who knew how long in the cold with wet clothes on. Instantly, my tone lightened. "You've got nothing to worry about."

"Thank you." A shiver wracked her body.

A crazy surge of possessiveness and caring washed through me. I fought my instinct to pull her against me and warm her with my body. Preferably naked.

We were quiet the rest of the short ride to my penthouse. When the doors started to slide open, Pria darted toward them so fast I thought she was going to run straight into them. She paused, looking over her shoulder the second her face would have slammed into the doors and gave a shaky, "thank you," before shooting into my apartment.

Giving her time, I slowly walked inside. I was immediately met with Orvy and Jimmy running and jumping up to greet me. I always loved how happy they were to see me when I arrived home. It didn't matter if I was gone for a day or a week, they were ecstatic to see me. I let Orvy place his paws on my shoulders and lick my face before I scratched behind his ears and then helped him down so I could greet Jimmy. He greeted me with equal fervor.

"All right, guys, let me get changed out of these wet clothes and I'll make you an early dinner." I started for my bedroom but decided to check on Pria. I didn't want her in her room beating herself up over losing Sarah or crying if she didn't believe me.

I headed to the guest room, ready to knock on the door, but found I didn't need to since it was slightly ajar. Imagine my shock when I found Pria slipping out of her jeans and could see everything through her wet, white T-shirt. Her brown nipples were hard peaks, her small breasts outlined within an inch of their life. I wanted nothing more than to cup them through the wet fabric and to feel the weight of them. To taste, bite, and suck on them. As she slipped her T-shirt over her head, I couldn't hold back any longer.

With quick strides, I had Pria in my arms, and I took her mouth in a desperate kiss. A kiss I'd wanted since the moment she stepped inside my office and saw my semi after jacking off to her in the bathroom before our meeting.

Her gasp was all I needed for me to slip my tongue inside and tangle with hers. My fingers slipped into her dark locks and fisted her hair. Pulling her by her tresses, I tilted her head to get a better angle. I couldn't get enough of her taste. It was a strange mix of cinnamon and honey that had me intoxicated. I knew from that first kiss I'd never have enough of Pria Wang.

My stubble from not shaving this morning scraped against her delicate skin marking it red. The sight only further turned me on. My other hand made its way to cup her bare breasts.

"King," she gasped my name. I wanted to hear it again and again and again. Pinching her nipple between my thumb and forefinger it hardened to the point it had to ache.

Pria's hands landed on my shoulders as she arched into my ministrations. "What are you doing?" she asked in a breathy whisper.

"Touching you." I kissed down her neck and across her collarbone. "Do you want me to stop?"

Pria shook her head as she ran her delicate fingers into my hair and pulled me closer. I took that as the signal she wanted more.

Before me, stood the most beautiful woman in the world. Normally, I wasn't one for small breasts, but I found Pria's fit perfectly in my mouth. I loved the taste of her skin and her soft flesh. Pulling her flush to me, she recoiled, and a shocked look crossed her face.

"What's wrong?" I asked as I tried to pull her back to me. Her trembling fingers met the buttons of my button-down and started to slip each out of their holes. It was then I realized I was just as soaked as she had been. It seemed she didn't like the cold fabric of my clothes. "You want me naked?" I smirked down at her. I definitely liked where this was going.

Looking up at me, her eyes narrowed as she pushed my shirt from my shoulders for it to fall down at our feet. I kicked it aside and started working on my belt first, and then the zipper of my slacks. Hearing Pria's breathing pick up as her gaze landed on my chest made my already stiff cock turn to granite. Stepping out of my pants and boxer briefs, my hands went back to Pria's soft skin as I guided her toward the bed.

I couldn't wait to be inside her, but she was tiny,

and I knew I had to prepare her for our first time. Running my hands up the inside of her thighs, I spread them wide and was shocked when her dripping wet lips were bare. Pria sat back on her elbows watching me with avid attention. I loved knowing she wanted to watch as much as I wanted to devour her.

Lying down between her legs, I licked my lips, knowing I was going to enjoy tasting her everywhere. Keeping my eyes on hers, I leaned down and bit the inside of her thigh. Not hard, but enough to make her jump and her breathing increase into sharp pants. "You drive me wild. From the moment I caught sight of you, I've wanted to defile your perfectly tight, little body and make it mine."

Instead of answering, Pria wound her fingers through my hair and guided me down to her promised land until my nose nudged her already hard clit. My tongue darted out, swiping up her center, and we both moaned. She was intoxicating. I vowed then and there, I wasn't going to stop until I left her boneless from orgasms with my mouth and fingers.

My thumbs parted her slick lips until her clit was bared to me. I hit it hard and fast. Keeping it exposed, I swirled my tongue around as my fingers dipped into her core. Hot and wet, she clamped down on my digits as I slowly moved them in and out of her.

Moaning my name and pushing me farther into her mound, I continued my assault on her bundle of nerves. Her body shuttered and I knew she was close to falling over the edge. Curling my fingers, I sucked her clit hard. I was rewarded with a thrashing Pria, arching her back and clamping her legs around my head while she chanted my name as she nearly pulled my hair out.

She let go, became unburdened and wild, and I couldn't wait to sink deep inside of her.

14

PRIA

HOLY FUCKING SHIT! DID THAT JUST HAPPEN? A NIP TO my inner thigh let me know I hadn't hit my head out on the street and imagined my boss going down on me.

Sliding up my body with his blond hair all a mess from my hands pulling and guiding him, King had a devilish grin adorning his handsome face. It really wasn't fair how amazing he looked at that moment or in general for that matter. Kingston Avery had it all. The looks, the body, the hair, brains, and money. And most definitely the cock.

Before I'd only caught a glimpse of it in his office and now that I felt the length and girth sliding along my leg, I knew King had a mega cock. When I say mega, I mean donkey dick huge. You know the kind you see in porn and you're scared for the girl. It was that kind of dick. Lord knew I'd watched a few a time or two, getting myself off after Haider left me blowing in the wind.

Now, I was the one who should be scared. I wasn't sure how he was going to fit inside of me. I wanted to laugh about the thought. I'd read in plenty of books where the heroine thought the same thing, but my body was used to something a whole lot smaller, and I was freaking out. All earlier pleasure was forgotten.

One of King's hands slid up my side while the other skated up my torso and between my breasts to rest at my collarbone. He must have seen the hesitance on my face.

"We don't have to do anything you're not comfortable with." His once heated look was gone and in its place was something I couldn't quite place. Was he annoyed by the thought he might not get laid after going down on me? Or did he think I hadn't enjoyed myself? Surely, he knew. There was no way to hide it as my legs trembled around his head or the wetness that was all around his mouth.

Placing a hand over his muscular shoulder, I tried to pull him down to me, but King wasn't having it. Instead, he sat back on his haunches making my arm fall down to my side on the bed.

"King," I gasped out his name, but had to stop as tears sprung to the back of my eyes. I faced the other way so he wouldn't see the wetness building in my eyes. After blinking a few times to rid myself of the moisture, I turned back to him. "I... it's not that I don't want you, because I do." I lifted my hand and trailed it down his chiseled chest. My fingers dipped between each ridge. "You're perfect. Maybe too perfect." I eyed his massive length and gulped. "God, this is so embarrassing."

"Don't tell me you're not a woman down there. I've been up close and personal, and you are most definitely a woman. You have the best smelling and tasting pussy lips I've ever had the pleasure of making my acquaintance with." A rogue grin tipped his lips. I wasn't sure if I wanted to smack or kiss the smirk off his handsome face.

"Nothing like that." I leaned up on an elbow feeling the need to be closer to him. "Have you ever had a woman tell you she wasn't a woman after you went down on her?" If I was in my right mind, I knew the answer to that question, and it was hell no. No woman would ever tell Kingston Avery that. He had probably been awesome at sex his first time. It took everything in me not to laugh. Why was I thinking like this at a time when all I should be thinking about was the insane body displayed in front of me?

He scoffed and continued to look down at me waiting for me to explain. My mouth opened and closed unsure if I could produce the words that needed to be said. "I'm having serious doubts about you being able to fit inside me. You're like porn star big."

King's head cocked to the side and a sexy smirk landed on his face. "You watch porn?" It wasn't a statement but a surprised question.

My elbow came out from under me and I fell back onto the bed. I rolled my eyes as I looked at his shocked expression. "On occasion, yes. I don't have some addiction to it or anything, but it's been needed on occasion with my ex. He was, to put it nicely, not as endowed as you." Not by a long shot.

"Obviously, or you wouldn't be freaking out." His hand went to his length and squeezed the base. "Trust me that I know what I'm doing. I promise I won't hurt you and you *will* stretch to fit me. Your vagina is meant to stretch."

"No shit, Sherlock, but no one is going to be giving me drugs to help me accommodate your cock."

Falling down to his side, King bellowed out a laugh so deep and loud he had the bed shaking. "Ms. Wang, you're good for the ego."

Like he needed his ego stroked. I rolled to my left side to watch him laugh. At the office, he was always so damn serious and pissed off looking; it was nice to see him let loose. I had a feeling the only place he let his guard down was at home or with his family. A tear slipped down his cheek from cracking up so hard. After a good two minutes of laughing, he calmed down, turning to face me with a broad smile. In one swift movement his arm wrapped around me and pulled me close before his hand lightly cupped my cheek. The tenderness in his eyes made me catch my breath. "I promise, I'll be gentle. I'd never do anything to intentionally hurt you unless you wanted me to." I opened my mouth, but he stopped me in my tracks. "Some like a little pain with sex."

I knew that. I'd never experienced it, but I'd read about it plenty. And then there was the porn. "Do you like pain?"

He looked up for a second. "I don't mind a woman digging her nails into my back as I bring her pleasure or a good tug of my hair." He smirked at me.

My faced heated at the memory of me pulling his hair while he was between my thighs. Lifting my right hand, I brushed his disheveled hair to the side. I liked knowing I had done that to him.

Pushing me onto my back, King hovered over me and swept my hair to the side. "You can tell me to stop at any time and I'll stop. Do you trust me to make this feel good for the both of us?" I nodded up at him. I'd agree to anything when his usual icy green eyes were warm and looking down at me the way they were.

Leaning down and kissing his way up my neck, my whole body lit up from the simple touch and a shudder of pleasure wracked my body. He pulled back to look down at me with tenderness and I swear I melted into a pile of goo. Wrapping my legs around his waist, I pulled King down to me and claimed his lips. They were unbelievably soft and full. I wanted to never stop kissing him while at the same time feel them over every inch of my body.

When two digits dipped inside, I gasped at how thick his fingers were. Taking advantage, King's tongue swept around my own. The kiss was slow and intoxicating. My arms wrapped around his broad shoulders wanting to feel his skin on mine.

Slipping another finger inside, my walls stretched and gripped onto King's fingers for purchase. It wasn't as uncomfortable as I thought it would be. It felt good, and I wanted more. Much more.

"I want you inside of me," I panted. My legs tightened around his middle, bringing him closer.

"In due time, my little troublemaker. You need to be prepared to take all of me." Dipping down, he sucked one of my breasts into his hot mouth and I moaned in pleasure. Holy hell what this man could do with his mouth and fingers. I couldn't wait to experience all of him. Even the thought sent an extra tingle of pleasure through my body. With each ministration, my body climbed higher and higher. My back arched off the bed, my legs fell to the sides to open up and feel more. Moving onto my other breast, King plucked my nipple before taking it in his mouth. It was as if my body had been waiting to get equal attention. Pleasure like I'd never known shot from the base of my neck down to my pulsing core.

King's fingers continued to pump in and out drawing every last ounce of pleasure from me while I moaned and gripped the sheet beneath me as if it could somehow ground me. When every last shudder had left my body, I opened my eyes to find King laid out beside me looking at me fondly. I wasn't sure why I was embarrassed after what he had just done to me, but I was.

This King confused me. How could he be so different outside of this apartment? Even when he was away on his trip, he had been gruff a majority of the time.

Not wanting to let silly insecurities take over, I moved to my side. One finger trailed along the arm that was resting between us. "Why are you looking at me like that?"

"Why wouldn't I? You're beautiful and even more so when you come."

I couldn't stop the broad smile that took over my face. It had been a long time since anyone had called me beautiful which was sad because up until last week, I'd been in what I thought was a loving relationship for years. It was amazing the signs you saw once your eyes were finally open wide.

"I want to watch you come."

His eyebrows rose and his face lit up. He looked so boyish in that moment that I had to sigh dreamily. Kingston Avery was going to ruin me. I just wasn't sure if it was going to be in the best way possible or my utter ruin.

"And I want you to watch me come repeatedly while I'm buried deep inside of you." Slipping a hand around my leg, King hiked it over his hip pulling us closer together. He was still hard and had been while giving me multiple orgasms, he had to be dying. His tip nudged my opening as his hand moved my leg up higher on his hip, opening me up farther to take him in. Inch by inch he slipped inside, pausing to let me become accustomed to his size.

"Fuck, Pria, you're so tight. I feel like I'm taking your virginity." He groaned as he held himself back.

"You kind of are," I joked. My arm tightened around his back as he stretched me. Leaning in, I kissed along his jaw. I needed a distraction and my lips on his body was the perfect way.

Dipping his head, King caught my lips as he surged the last few inches into me. I whimpered into his mouth as my walls stretched to accommodate him. "I don't think I'm going to last long. Fuck, your boyfriend must have been small," he said on a groan as he slowly pulled out to the tip.

I hadn't known what I was missing until now, but King was right. Haider was tiny compared to him. I laughed at the thought as he unhurriedly drove back in.

"Now's not the time to laugh." He growled out before sucking the lobe of my ear. He had to have known I wasn't laughing at him. Nothing about King was funny, especially what he was making me feel. Before I'd been lucky to have an orgasm during sex, so I didn't think it was possible to have more than one in such a short period of time, but as King filled me with each glorious inch of him, pressure started to build up in me once again.

"I'm going to come again." I whimpered, holding him closer. Our position was so intimate. Not at all what I was expecting for our first time. Not that I was expecting us to ever have sex or that we would ever again, but it was a nice surprise, nonetheless.

"That's the point." He grunted. Each sensual slide of his hips stirred awake something deep inside. I was never going to get enough of this man. His hard exterior and the soft, caring man buried deep down that I'd caught glimpses of.

"Come with me, Pria." His thumb found my clit and rubbed slow, delicious circles as he kept slowly filling me. Shattering in his arms, I called out his name like a prayer. He was now my god and if he made me feel like this, I'd happily worship him night and day. Every nerve ending in my body sang his praise.

Swallowing my cry, King's mouth met mine in a hot, slow kiss. Everything was heavenly timed to the tempo of his hips. I clung to him as if my life depended on it as I slowly came down. King's hips picked up speed, but not the driving force I'd expected from him before he stilled deep inside of me. Our mouths broke apart as he breathed a deep groan against my lips. I watched in fascination as his face tightened in pleasure and slowly went lax, his full lips brushing against mine in tenderness.

It was single-handedly the sexiest thing I'd ever experienced, and I couldn't wait to do it again. Except there wouldn't be another time because I couldn't have sex with my boss. Not only was it against company policy, and I liked my job, but I knew he'd only break my heart because after one time, I had already started to fall for him.

15

PRIA

Hot.

Sweltering fire.

Those were my first thoughts as I woke up with the sun beaming down on my face. I tried to throw the plush comforter off me but was stopped by a lead weight on top of the covers. Upon further inspection, I realized it was King's arm. My boss's arm. My very naked boss, who was plastered against me.

King moaned from beside me, tightening his arm around my waist. His voice was full of gravel and oh so sexy from misuse. "Go back to sleep. It's too early." He nuzzled his nose into the back of my neck. Even though it felt wonderful, it also increased my body temperature. I swear I could feel beads of sweat pop up all along my back. "Trust me, the dogs won't let us sleep in too late. By the way, when did Orvy break in?"

I wasn't used to cuddling, and in the past, I'd thought I wasn't missing anything, but I couldn't bear to break from King's hold no matter how hot I was. To say I was shocked would be an understatement. Maybe that's where Orvy got his need to cuddle from. I thought I'd wake up to King fleeing my bed or already alone, but he'd stayed with me, wrapped around me the entire night. Freeing my foot from our entangled legs, I inched it past Orvy's big body on the other side of me and out of the blankets to get some fresh air in an attempt to cool down.

"I'm not sure, but I know I didn't let him in. Did you?"

King's arms tightened around me as he laughed into the nape of my neck. "Obviously not."

"If you didn't let him in and I didn't... I think he's figured out how to get in."

"I probably forgot to lock the door. He hates sleeping by himself and is desperate enough." Resting his cheek on my shoulder, he huffed out. "No more talking. Sleep."

I'd try, but sleeping with these two was like being in a furnace. A very soft and lovable furnace, but a furnace, nonetheless. One that I knew I shouldn't get used to.

CUTTING UP SOME FRUIT FOR MY BREAKFAST, I YELPED and almost cut my finger when Sarah nudged my hip and then trotted off with her nose in the air. I guess King was back with the dogs.

"Woman, you are dangerous to sleep with." King chuckled from behind me. "I literally had to pin you down so I wouldn't get elbowed or smacked in the face." So he had willingly stayed the night. That was good to know. He could have easily left after the first jab.

"I'm sorry. I should have warned you, but I thought..." I bit my bottom lip from telling him I thought he was a love 'em and leave 'em kind of guy.

"Finish what you were going to say, Ms. Wang."

Ms. Wang.

Was he back to being my boss? This was definitely going to make things awkward at the office.

Tipping my chin up, I turned to face him. "I thought you'd leave."

"You'd be right. Usually I do." He shrugged.

Why'd he call me out on it if it was his typical behavior? I guess he was back to being his usually cocky self.

He poured himself a cup of coffee from his crazy coffee maker I hadn't even bothered to touch while he was gone. "Tonight, we'll sleep in my bed. I've got my blinds on a timer and they open extra late on the weekends." I bit my bottom lip again. "What?" he growled, annoyed.

"There's no tonight. Now that you're home, I'm not really needed here. So, I was planning to stay at a hotel until I find a new place, which has proved to be more difficult than I thought it would be." Mostly because I hadn't even started to look.

"Stay here until you find a place," he said nonchalantly. "I have to go out of town for multiple business meetings and you can watch the dogs."

"You still want me to watch them?" Was he desperate? He had to be because just yesterday I'd lost one of his dogs.

"Why not? You know what to do and I'll need someone who knows them." He sipped his coffee, giving me a one shoulder shrug.

Who was this man and what had he done with my boss?

"Why don't you want me to leave? I'll probably end up killing or losing one of your dogs if I'm left with them again. You can find better than me."

Placing his coffee on the counter, King stalked toward me and put his hands on either side of me, boxing me in. I strained to look up as he looked down. Our height difference was comical, especially when I was without my heels, but somehow it worked extremely well for us in bed. King seemed to be thinking something along those lines. He picked me up and placed me on the counter, spreading my legs wide to stand between them. "I don't think I'll find anyone better than you. I like you and my dogs like you, and I have a feeling you like us too." His large hands cradled my hips as he smiled down at me. I watched his perfectly pink, kissable lips form each word wanting to trap them between my teeth. "I like how small you are, shorty, and how sexy you look on my countertop. I may have to lay you out on top of it and have my wicked way with you."

"I like the sound of that." No longer able to hold myself back, I leaned up and sucked King's bottom lip into my mouth before giving it a nip.

One of King's hands slid underneath the T-shirt I had slipped on after getting out of bed. He was nice enough to take the dogs out and let me stay behind. "Tell me you'll stay. Let's have a fun weekend only getting out of bed to eat and let the dogs out. Maybe we can set the world record for the most orgasms in seventy-two hours."

I wasn't sure which I wanted to do more. Roll my eyes or laugh at him and his huge ego. Yes, King was talented, but thinking he could set the record was a little much. Leaning back on my elbows, I smiled up at him. "Do you know the record number?"

"If you're willing to try, I'll look it up so we have a goal to strive for. I'm thinking..." he hummed to himself with a mischievous grin on his uber handsome face, "one hundred orgasms in a weekend." One finger rubbed my inner thigh driving me wild while the other hand inched up toward my breasts. It was so close yet so far away.

"You're crazy." I quirked my head to the side. "Is that a hundred between the two of us or just me? Never mind because either way, I think I'd probably die. Although, death by orgasm doesn't sound bad."

King's hand left from between my legs to grip my hip. "Stop overthinking it. Sex with you was..." He seemed to be unable to find the right word. Had it been bad? No, it couldn't have been, otherwise, he wouldn't want to spend the rest of the weekend in bed. Unless he was taking pity on me and thought he needed to teach me a few things. I wasn't opposed to more amazing sex with King, but I didn't want it to be a pity fuck either.

He ground his teeth together as he looked down at me. "I can see the wheels turning, Pria. Don't think I do this often, or ever as a matter of fact."

Have sex with women all weekend? I was certain he did, and it wouldn't surprise me if it was with more than one woman.

"Stop thinking and just let me talk. Listen, because I'm going to say this one time only. I don't talk about my feelings. *Ever*. I don't date, do girl-friends or friends with benefits, or anything of the kind. I don't say nice things afterward or talk about my sex life. *When* I have sex," a muscle twitched in his jaw, "it's a one-time deal. I don't cuddle or stay the night, and I most definitely don't bring them here."

Why was he telling me all this?

"I'm telling you this because..." King let out a frustrated breath. Could he read my mind, or had I said that out loud? "You're hot, your body is banging, and our sex last night was different than anything I've ever had. Not in a bad way, don't get me wrong. It sparked something inside of me and I want to continue to explore whatever it is."

I sat flabbergasted at his admission. I was sure I looked like an idiot, but he didn't comment on it. What did he want from me if he didn't do fuck buddies or girlfriends? Finally, I got my wits about me or so I thought and blurted out. "We did have great chemistry."

"We *do* so what do you say about me fucking you on my countertop?"

My hand went to the growing bulge in his tight jeans and gave it a squeeze. "It sounds like the perfect way to spend my weekend." What I didn't say was how I wanted to know what would happen after this weekend was over since Kingston Avery didn't fuck anyone more than once. I wanted to know more and ask questions, but I knew he wouldn't answer them. The time for talking was over.

"Perfect, Ms. Wang." King wasted no time in stripping the shirt from my body. His large hands caressed my now overheated skin as his eyes devoured me. "You're perfect."

His words emboldened me. It was my turn to remove his clothes. Grabbing his white T-shirt by the hem, I lifted it over his head and threw it to the floor. I spotted Sarah standing there staring at us, but I didn't care as long as she left us alone. Undoing his jeans, I slipped my hand inside his gray boxer briefs and wrapped my hand around his steel shaft.

"How does your touch…" He groaned deep in his throat when I squeezed his tip. His eyes closed in ecstasy. I wanted to pull him on top of me and learn every inch of his body. Before I could move, King pulled away to shuck off his tennis shoes, socks, and jeans. He stood before me in only his boxers and I took in every flawless inch of him from his broad imposing shoulders, the lean muscular legs of a runner, even down to his bare sexy feet. Feet weren't meant to be sexy but his were.

Lifting one foot, I checked my pink painted toenails. I wanted Kingston Avery to find my feet as sexy as I found his. Slipping his thumbs into the waistband of his boxers, King slowly dragged them down over his long legs. When he stood up, his cock bobbed and settled against his stomach. My mouth watered at the sight of him.

I didn't have to wait long. King grabbed my foot and brought it up to his mouth placing a kiss on my arch before he placed it on his shoulder. He gave the same treatment to my other foot, leaving me spread wide for him.

Swiping a finger through my pussy, King brought it up to his mouth and tasted me. "Fuck, you taste good. I'm going to eat you for breakfast later, but right now I have to be inside of you." Sliding two fingers inside, he only pumped twice before pulling out. "You're so wet and ready for me. Perfect."

Gripping his length, King ran it up and down my folds before gliding only the tip inside all the while watching. I wanted to force the rest of him in, but his hands had moved to hold my ankles leaving me immobile. He moved his hips torturously slow as he filled me, letting me get accustomed to his size. Only once he was all the way inside did he look up at me. "This is going to be fast and I want you to come with me so play with yourself. Touch yourself as if it were my hands on you."

Holy hell that was hot. My core spasmed from his words alone. I did as I was directed. One hand went to my breasts to twist and pinch my nipples while the other skated down my flat stomach. Instead of touching myself, I ran the tip of one finger down

King's blond treasure trail until I reached the base of his cock.

"I can't hold back much longer." His voice was husky and deeper than normal.

I wanted to touch him more, but I also wanted him to start moving. To feel the exquisite pleasure of him filling me over and over again. Running my fingers up my slit, I started rubbing fast circles as King pulled back and slammed into me. I had to stop and catch my breath. I'd never experienced anything rough and dominant, but I was finding I liked anything Kingston Avery did to me.

His left hand moved from my ankle and slapped the side of my ass causing me to yelp. "I won't tell you again. Touch yourself. This is going to be rough and quick." As if to punctuate his point, he pulled out nearly to the tip and slammed into me. Only this time he didn't stop for me to catch my breath. Instead, his pace quickened as he fucked me harder, never letting up. His breathing picked up speed and his arms flexed as he drew closer and closer to his orgasm.

My fingers circled my bundle of nerves at a furious pace as I tried to keep up. I had a feeling if I didn't get off on my own this round, King wouldn't help me. I'm not sure where this side of him came from, but I liked seeing him take control of his pleasure and mine.

"Fuck, I like watching you pleasure yourself. Do you have a vibrator or something? I want to watch you fuck yourself." The muscles in his neck tightened as he pistoned into me like his balls were on fire.

The thought of King watching me as I used my vibrator on myself sent me over the edge. I'd always hidden that part of myself from Haider, and the fact that King wanted to watch had my digits swirling around my clit faster as I called out his name.

Letting my legs fall to the side, King pulled me up until we were chest to chest as I milked his cock. I slumped against his heaving chest as I caught my own breath, my arms loosely draped around him.

I was so relaxed I was about asleep until King jerked back making his cock slip out of me. Turning my head to see what was going on, I found Sarah resting her head on King's ass.

"For fuck's sake, Sarah, go lie down." Lifting her snout in the air, she pranced out of the kitchen. King looked pissed as he watched her go.

"She doesn't like me." I giggled trying to break the tension. Only a moment ago we had been in the afterglow of bliss.

"Too bad because I do." King picked me up and placed me gently down on the floor and took my hand in his. "Let's go break in my bed."

I couldn't think of anything I wanted more.

16

PRIA

"I think that's one hundred," I panted out.

"That's twenty at best." His hot breath fanned across my neck with his low chuckle.

"Whatever number it is, I need a break. Your stamina is commendable." My hand ran across his shoulder and down his side. "Are you even human?"

He smirked at me. "How about we take a nap after I take the dogs out?"

"Do you want me to come?" I really hoped he said no because I didn't think I had the energy to get out of bed.

King nuzzled into my neck. "Thank you for offering, but I'll let you get some rest."

"How are you not tired? I'm not that much older than you." I couldn't understand how he seemed to have an endless amount of energy.

"I work out regularly. How often do you exercise?"

I was lucky I was naturally skinny with the way I ate, but I didn't have muscles or stamina and it was showing after the workout he'd given me. "I think the last time I ran was in high school gym class."

"Well, you might want to start if you want to keep up with me." His lips lightly brushed the side of my neck as if to lighten his words.

"I don't think all the exercise in the world would help me keep up with you."

"Maybe not, but it can't hurt. If you want, you can come to the gym with me. There's one in the building here."

I was surprised he didn't have one in his apartment. He definitely had enough space for one. "When do you have time to work out?" From what I've witnessed, King was one of the first at work and the last to leave.

"I don't need a lot of sleep, so I get up early, take the dogs for a walk, sometimes I take Sarah and Orvy for a run, and then hit the gym for some weight training." It showed too.

I liked my sleep too much to get up early to workout. It was all I could do to keep my eyes open at the moment, but I liked talking to King so I pushed through the exhaustion. Even though he said he didn't open up to anyone, he didn't seem to have a problem talking to me and letting little snippets about his life slip.

His lips trailed down my neck and across my shoulder. "When we wake up, I want you to sit on my face and come all over it."

Hello! That woke me up. I loved all the dirty ways King wanted me. He made me realize I was lucky Haider had cheated on me because never once in our relationship did we have sex like this. I think King had given me more orgasms in one day than my three years with Haider.

"I heard your heart pick up. You like the sound of that, don't you?" His teeth nipped the curve of my shoulder.

"Very much so." It was a little embarrassing my body gave me away so easily. Now that he'd mentioned our next time, I needed to bring up birth control and condoms. Every time I'd tried, he deflected with his mouth in a strategic place. While I loved every ounce of pleasure he'd given me, I wouldn't love it if he gave me an STD. "King." I started off, moving onto my side as best as I could and wrapped my arms around him in an attempt to keep him from fleeing.

"Yes, Pria?" The arm draped around my waist gave me a little squeeze.

I wasn't sure how to say it so I did it the only way I could. I blurted out the words and then wanted to bury my head into my pillow. "I thought I should put it out there, but we haven't used a condom."

Without any effort on his part, King slipped out of my arms to lean on his elbow and look down at me with an unreadable expression on his face. "I'm aware."

I narrowed my eyes at him. "I don't want an STD."

"Neither do I."

I huffed. Why was he being so obtuse? "We didn't discuss our sex life and I haven't had a chance to get tested since I found out that my ex was cheating on me."

King's brows furrowed. "I hadn't thought about that. Do you think he gave you anything?"

"I don't know," I exclaimed a little too loudly. In all actuality, I hadn't thought about it until now. "I didn't think he'd cheat on me in the first place. The only saving grace is that it had been a few months since we'd slept together, but who knows what that hussy gave him."

King dipped down and laughed into my neck. He seemed to like it and spent a great deal of time there. "Hussy? That's what you call her?"

"Do you have a better word?" Now I was getting annoyed.

"Bitch? Slut? I can think of more words that are from this decade."

"Ha, ha. You're so funny. But really none of this is funny. Even if Haider didn't give me anything, you very well could."

His laser like green eyes narrowed into slits at me. "Is that what you think of me? That I'm a walking STD?"

"No, of course, I don't, but I don't know where you've been. You've got the reputation of a womanizer. And while you're great and all, I'm not ready for a baby."

King sputtered next to me. "A baby?"

"Yes, you do know how babies are made don't you?" And here I thought he was smart.

King rolled his eyes at me. It looked so foreign on his face. "Yes, I know how babies are made." I continued to look up at him waiting for him to say more and watched as his eyes widened. His throat bobbed as he swallowed. "Are you not on birth control?"

"Yes, I'm on the pill, but it's not one hundred percent effective. I would have appreciated if you wouldn't have blocked me every time I tried to ask you about it. Each time you touched me, my body betrayed me, and I forgot all about being safe. Now that you've dumped your cum in me half a dozen times, I thought it would be smart for us to have the talk."

King rolled over until he was hovering over me,

looking me in the eyes with his laser like focus. "Contrary to what others say, I don't sleep around. When I was younger, I can admit I was a bit of a womanizer, but that got old when the women I slept with wanted more." I wanted to ask what more they wanted, and it must have shown because King answered my unspoken question after letting out a frustrated breath. "Either they wanted more attention than I was willing to give, which wasn't much, I'll be honest, or they wanted me to spend money on them for fucking them. I don't play that way. The worst were the ones who used me to get ahead any way they could. They weren't worth the hassle. You know the hours I work." He gave a half shrug. "It's easier all the way around for me to use my hand."

King smirked down at me. I wasn't sure what to think. It seemed unfathomable that he jacked off instead of using any number of women at his disposal. I believed him though. What I wasn't sure of was if I was there because I was convenient and he was tired of using his hand or if he liked me. I hated being insecure like that, but I was thanks to my ex. I felt as if I couldn't trust my instincts about men. I didn't want to be wrong about another one. King had to know I wasn't using him. No one could know that I fucked my boss for a weekend. Which was all it ever could be. Just one glorious weekend with orgasms galore.

"If it makes you feel better, I've used protection with every woman I've ever been with."

Now it was my turn for my eyes to narrow. "Are you only saying that to make me feel better or are you telling the truth?"

"One thing you'll learn about me is that I always tell the truth. Even if it will hurt your feelings, I always tell it like it is. I don't like liars."

"Neither do I."

"Good, now you know I'll never lie to you and I expect you'll never lie to me." King was back to being the man I was used to at the office. He was commanding and serious.

"I won't. I promise," I vowed softly as I looked up at him.

"Good." He nodded down at me before he stood. King's mouth was downturned, our moment ruined. "Get some sleep."

I watched him walk away, his toned ass flexing with every step. Even dead tired and fully sated, seeing King naked before me had me wanting him again. Everything about him was all male and perfect. In a way, it made me sad thinking King probably thought he had to be perfect at all times, no matter the circumstances. Yes, I was reaping the rewards, but I also wanted to see his flaws. Inside and out. I wanted him to let his guard down and just be King. The man who had the face of a sweet, gorgeous boy and not the guarded man moving away from me.

I must have fallen asleep while thinking about the King he showed everyone because the next time I blinked my eyes open it was dark in the room and the man himself was spooned up behind me with his arm draped around my waist and his hand cupping my breast.

Slowly turning in his arms so I didn't wake him up, I stopped when I was face-to-face with King. I was shocked to see how young and peaceful he looked while asleep. His long lashes fanned out across his cheeks and his lips were slightly parted letting out little puffs of air. I wanted to trace my finger over his straight nose and high cheekbones, but I held myself back, so I didn't wake him. Kingston may have acted as if he wasn't tired, but it was obvious he'd been more worn out than either of us had thought.

My eyes trailed to his messy blond hair that hung over his forehead, stopping back over his angelic face, and then down over to the bronzed skin of his torso. King had a light smattering of hair on his chest and stomach that I wanted to run my finger through. Everything about him had me falling under his spell. I couldn't let myself turn into a lovesick fool and I knew I most certainly shouldn't have had sex with him. Maybe I should have packed my stuff and got the hell out of there before he woke up. I could have sucked it up and stayed with my dad and Lao Lao until I found a place. What I really needed to do was tell him that I knew his family.

"I can feel you staring at me," King grumbled.

My cheeks flushed with embarrassment. I'd been so lost in my own thoughts, I hadn't noticed him wake up. "Sorry, I was trying to figure out what to do."

"To do about what?" His left eye opened to peek out at me before he closed it again.

"Pack up and leave or—"

King's eyes flashed open. "What do you mean, leave? I thought we were having a fun weekend."

"We are or were, but we aren't being smart. I'm having sex with my boss and the more I'm around you the more... I don't know. I guess the more I like you. You're likable most of the time and I don't want to get fired or hate you when this all turns to shit." I blurted the last part out in a fast breath.

"Why do you think it will all turn to shit? I'm not going to fire you, Pria." He blew out a frustrated breath. "We're both adults and can handle anything bad that may come and act amicably, don't you think?"

"I agree, but I'm not sure if I can keep myself from feeling things for you. You have heartbreak written all over you and I just got out of a serious relationship."

"Okay, slow down. I'm not going to break your heart and I'm well aware of when your last relationship ended. How about we make a deal? If you start to feel things that you don't want to feel, we stop having sex even if you haven't found a place to stay. Things will go back to usual and you'll still have your job."

"How do you have all the answers? Aren't you worried I'll turn into some crazy stalker and steal your dogs?"

"Are you worried you'll fall for them too?" He grinned, not taking me seriously. No, I wouldn't run off with his dogs or stalk him, but I could easily fall for him. I already had for his amazing cock and mouth. "It's the weekend. Relax. It's an order from your boss and you should always do what he says."

I smiled at him, letting it all go. He was right. I was taking everything too seriously. It was time I enjoy myself, and Kingston Avery was, without fail, the best person for me to take pleasure in. I brushed my lips against his. "I should, should I?"

"Yes, Ms. Wang, you should. I believe you had a date on my face. What do you say you fuck my mouth and then we'll get some takeout and watch a movie?"

Perfect. "Sounds like a date."

17

KINGSTON

FROM THE CORNER OF MY EYE, I SPOTTED PRIA WINCE from her corner of the couch. I wasn't sure what the wince or the distance on the couch was about. My mouth had touched every inch of her body. After that level of intimacy, I couldn't understand why she chose to sit so far away from me. Was it my speech earlier about not letting anyone get close to me and not doing girlfriends? Was that why she had wanted to leave when I woke up?

Orvy nudged Pria's leg, making her shift in her seat and this time she couldn't hide the look of pain on her face.

"Orvy, go lie down," I commanded. I had a feeling my dear, Ms. Wang had spoiled the other residents of my penthouse while I was gone. Hell, she was spoiling me. My sex life would never be the same.

"He's fine. Maybe he needs to go out. I can take him." Gingerly she tried to get up.

"You're not taking him anywhere like that. What the hell happened? Did you fall down at some point and I missed it?"

Clutching a pillow to her chest, she laughed without humor. "I believe I fell on your dick one too many times, Mr. Avery."

Hearing Pria call me Mr. Avery while only in my T-shirt made my dick twitch. Had I been too rough earlier? Sitting up a little straighter, I asked concerned, "Did I hurt you?"

Pria waved me off. "You didn't do anything but give me a good time. The problem is the only thing that's been shoved up my vagina in the last three years was no bigger than a tampon."

I blinked back at her words. Surely the ex was bigger than that, but given how tight she was, not by much.

"Does that mean sex is off the table for the rest of the weekend?"

Her eyes turned to slits. "Oh my God, King. What is with you and wanting to have sex all weekend?"

Because it was great and felt fantastic.

"I swear you're trying to get me pregnant."

What the hell was she talking about? We'd already talked about birth control and she swore she was on the pill.

"I thought you said you were—"

"I am, but it's like you want to defeat the odds by coming in me as many times as possible."

"I could pull out and come on you if that will make you feel better." Now that the thought was in my head, I did like the idea of coating her skin with my cum.

Her eyes darkened. It seemed Ms. Wang liked the thought as much as I did. "That's not the point."

"Pria, you act as if your birth control has an expiration date. You do know how it works right? It's not as if, when you have sex by some magical number say one hundred, you'll get pregnant that time."

She rolled her eyes at me. "I do know how it works and I'm sorry, I don't want to fight. I know you don't want a child with me." She sighed, rubbing Orvy between the ears. He hadn't stopped laying his head on her leg and staring up at her. "I feel like a failure because my body couldn't handle your dick."

"You're not a failure. I shouldn't have pushed it, especially when I knew how tight you are. How long has it been since you've had sex?" She'd mentioned it had been a while, but I wasn't sure how long that entailed.

"With a dick as big as yours? Never. With any dick? Six months. How long has it been since you had sex?" Her eyes gleamed. I had a feeling she'd wanted to know this answer before but was afraid I wouldn't answer.

I thought back to the last time I'd had sex. It had been quite some time. "Probably five or six months."

Pria sputtered and coughed, seeming to choke on the air. She looked at me with wide brown eyes in disbelief, but she knew I was telling the truth. What she couldn't believe is that I'd gone that long without sticking my dick in someone. I'd gone longer, but I wouldn't tell her that. If it wasn't for the woman who sat in front of me, my celibacy streak would still be going strong.

A look of clarity came upon her face. "Ah, now I understand. I'm sorry to let you down, but we're going to have to slow down and give my vajayjay a break."

What the hell? "Is your pussy this vajayjay you're talking about?"

"Yes, King. Not everyone calls it a pussy."

"Would you rather I refer to it as your cunt?"

"No, I would not." Her tone turned serious and slightly pissed off. She didn't like the word cunt. Not many women did.

"So, can I continue to call it your pussy because there's no way in hell I'm going to call it *that?*"

"You may." She laughed and her entire face lit up. I didn't think Pria had any idea how beautiful she was. Her tool of an ex had no idea what he had given up, but that was fine with me because now I got the pleasure of seeing her face brighten, whether it be from sex or from simple words.

"Is there anything that will make you feel better down there?" I gestured between her legs. She may have said I could continue to call it her pussy, but I knew she didn't love the word, and I hated calling it a vagina. It was too technical.

Pria cocked her head to the side, looking over at me with her lips tipped up. "You do have that big tub in your bathroom. Perhaps a soak in some warm water will help alleviate my symptoms."

"Are you sure you don't just want to get into my big tub?" I joked. I'd seen her eye it with longing every time she was in the bathroom.

"I'm not going to lie and say I don't want to take a test run in it because I do. It's big enough to be a small swimming pool. I bet you haven't set foot in it."

"And you'd be right. Give me a few minutes and I'll get it ready for you."

"You don't have to do that."

"I did just brutalize you with my cock; it's the least I can do." For some strange reason, I wanted to do something nice for her, and it had nothing to do with if I made her feel better, I'd get to fuck her some more.

Slipping the blanket off the back of the couch, I

draped it over Pria and headed to get her bath ready. After turning the dual faucets on, I scavenged my cabinets for anything that could be used as bubble bath. Women liked bubble baths, didn't they? Much to my dismay, I had nothing that could produce bubbles of any kind. I'd have to rectify that when I made my next grocery order because I planned to be inside Pria Wang as much as possible for as long as she'd let me.

Once the water was filled a little over halfway, I went back into the living room to find Orvy and Jimmy up on the couch, on each side of Pria. They looked comfortable and like it wasn't their first time up on the couch.

All three of them seemed to notice me at the same time. Orvy and Jimmy jumped down from the couch looking guilty and Pria flinched as she stood. She was the guiltiest out of the bunch, but I couldn't even be mad at her. I loved how much she seemed to care for my dogs, and I knew they loved her. Well, not Sarah, but she was a hard nut to crack. It wasn't that my trio of four-legged friends didn't like other people, but they didn't snuggle up to anyone but me. Until now.

"I'm so sorry, King. They jumped up to see me and I couldn't tell them no. They're just too sweet."

"Your bath is ready." I turned on my heel and left.

I wasn't going to mention how I doubted it was the first time.

I laid a towel and robe out for her to use once she was finished. I wasn't sure what I was going to do while she soaked in the tub. I always had work to be done, but there was something about Pria that made me want to live my life even doing the simplest of things instead of spending almost every waking moment working.

Pria stepped in the room and I swear her eyes got glassy. One hand covered her mouth as the other went to her chest. She took in the candles I'd lit around the room. Thank you, Mom, for stocking up on them for me. Too bad she hadn't put any bubble bath or oils in here, but the candles seemed to do the trick.

"King you didn't have to do all this," she whispered.

"I know I didn't. I don't do anything I don't want to do."

"All the same, thank you, this was very sweet of you." She walked over to the tub and dipped her hand into the water. A small smile graced her face.

Stepping out of the way, I headed toward the door. "If you need anything yell."

"You're leaving?"

"Did you want me to watch?" Kinky.

Pria chewed on the inside of her cheek for a

second before she started to slip out of the T-shirt she was wearing. "You could join me."

The moment her breasts came into view, I removed my clothes like a madman. It wasn't my finest moment, but it was honest. I wanted Pria anyway I could get her.

I watched her step into the warm water and slink down until the water mostly covered her. It would take a few more minutes before the tub was full. A contented sigh left her lips as she stretched out and floated in the water for a moment. Sitting up, she leaned back into the curved shape of the bathtub and closed her eyes. "Are you going to join me or were you planning to stand naked and jerk yourself off while I enjoyed the warm water?"

I wouldn't be opposed to watching her, but I decided to do that another time. Stepping inside, I sat down on the other end to give her room to relax. I stretched my legs out with Pria's legs in the middle of mine. "I wouldn't mind watching you and pleasuring myself, but I'd much rather be inside of you or have those perfect lips of your around my cock."

Pria's cheeks pinked up, but I saw her eyes darken.

"I'd like to taste you." She stopped abruptly.

"But?" I knew there was more, but I had no idea what it could possibly be.

Pria huffed and splashed water at me. Instead of

retaliating I waited patiently knowing she'd eventually tell me. Pria Wang might get embarrassed, but she wasn't a coward.

"We've already discussed how large you are and it's kind of annoying we have to do it again. I mean really your ego doesn't need to be any bigger than it already is."

"What are you..." Then what she was saying finally occurred to me. "Are you very experienced in giving head?"

"I've given plenty but with something much smaller."

I hated how much it pissed me off hearing of another man's cock in her mouth. The thought of her pretty pink lips wrapped around some other guy's member made me want to hunt him down and kill him. But I also loved knowing he was tiny and hadn't pleased her in bed in any way. That pleasure was all mine.

"So, you're afraid it won't all fit? I can assure you that it won't. You use your hand and mouth. I won't shove it down your throat no matter how much I may want to. I'm also not into gagging women with my cock. I don't want to see your tears." I didn't want to see Pria's tears, I had, in fact, made women take me down their throats and watched tears slipped down their cheeks without my usual response to a woman crying. I knew it was different, but still, I couldn't do it to Pria unless she begged me to. If she begged I would never deny her.

"I've only ever been with Chinese men." Why was she telling me this? "In our culture, we don't talk about sex with our parents or our partners. While I may have thought I was experienced before you got me in your bed, I now know I am not." She bit her bottom lip before she slipped under the water.

I tried to wait for her to come up and finish what she was saying, but Pria either could hold her breath for an extremely long time or she was trying to drown herself so she didn't have to finish talking. I gave her another couple of seconds before I scooped her out of the water and into my lap.

"What the hell, Pria? Would you rather die than tell me whatever it was you were going to say?"

She wiped the water out of her eyes and then looked me square in the eye. "I may not seem shy and I'm not, but I'm not accustomed to speaking this way. It's a lot for me. If I'm doing something wrong, I want you to show me how to do it the right way. I don't want to disappoint you."

My heart actually ached from her words. Had I somehow made Pria feel as if anything she had done wasn't wonderful? Because every single sexual experience with her had been great. More than great. If I was honest with myself, it was the best I'd experienced with anyone. I wasn't sure how, but we were perfect together sexually.

Pria dipped low in the water and started to giggle. Her eyes dancing with mischief.

I felt my brows pull down in confusion. "What's so funny?"

"I don't know how a man can look simultaneously uncomfortable and aroused at the same time."

"Is that how I look?" Pria nodded, giggling. I looked down through the water at my erection. "No bubbles lead to transparency and I like what I see."

"So do I. Have you ever taken a bath?" She started to rub her hand up and down my calf. The feeling of her hands on me was nice and relaxing.

"Everyone's taken a bath in their life." My tone was terse. I didn't want to go down that road, but obviously, Pria didn't hear it or chose to ignore it.

"When was the last time you took a bath?"

"I don't know," I answered annoyed even though I knew exactly when it was. Murphy had gotten sick. Too sick for my parents to have time to even give me a bath and demanded I start taking showers.

"Okay, that's fine. I can distinctly remember the day I stopped and started taking showers. Although we always put our feet in the tub to wash our feet before bed if we didn't bathe."

Weird.

"Don't give me that look." She splashed water at

me again. "Have you ever taken a bath with a woman before?"

"If I had, do you think I'd look so uncomfortable?"

"I don't know." She closed her eyes and continued to rub my leg. "You might if it had been a bad experience, but I'm going to stop asking you questions about it and say you haven't taken a bath with anyone before. I like being a first for you."

So did I.

I relaxed back as well now that she promised to stop asking questions. "I'm putting bubbles on the next shopping list."

"So, I take it there will be more baths in your future. Will I be a part of them or—"

"It will be you, Pria. I don't bring women into my home. I told you that. How about I ask you some questions?"

"Fire away."

"Have you taken a bath with anyone before?"

"I think what you really want to know is if I've taken one with a man, and the answer is no. Why would I when no one made my lady bits ache like you?"

I wanted to ask if she'd taken one with a woman just to get a rise out of her, but I held my tongue. "I'd say I'm sorry, but I'm not. Not when we've had all this amazing sex." A smile spread across her face at the mention of our sex.

"Me too. I can't believe you've never put someone out of commission before. I mean, damn, you couldn't just have girth, but you've got length as well. You've got a monster cock."

I was glad she thought so.

"Damn straight."

18

KINGSTON

IT TOOK ALL MY WILLPOWER NOT TO FOLLOW PRIA OUT of the elevator and into her office after our weekend together. I wasn't done with her. Not by a long shot. All the way up the elevator, I fantasized about bending her over my desk and taking her from behind.

I wasn't sure where my need to be inside of her during every waking minute came from. I couldn't count how many times I'd unloaded inside her over the weekend, and I'd lost track of how many orgasms I'd given her. Whatever it was I wanted to do it every weekend. Nothing was better than being deep inside Pria's tight heat.

The intercom buzzed before my new secretary's voice interrupted my fantasy. Her name was Cindy or Sandy. I couldn't remember. She started working here right before my last business trip and it seemed after me being gone, she thought her job was to sit on the phone and talk to whoever it was she talked to. She was annoyed anytime she had to actually work. I was in search of a new secretary and she knew it so that didn't help her attitude toward me.

I wasn't sure why she acted the way she did when I was her boss and the owner of the company. Did she not realize how easily I could fire her? Still, I'd wait until I had a replacement. I needed someone to at least answer my phone so I could get some work done.

"Mr. Avery," Cindy or Sandy's nasally voice came over the intercom. "A Mr. Whitmore is on the line for you. He says it's urgent."

If it was anyone other than Whitmore, I wouldn't have taken the call. Hitting the button for line one, I put him on speakerphone so I could continue to type my email. "Whitmore, what can I do for you?"

"Mr. Avery, I just got off the phone with someone at Sun Heights Investments. Their CEO had a heart attack last night and they're wanting to sell as fast as possible. We need to grab it before any other companies get wind of what happened."

Who's to say they hadn't?

"What do we know about them? Have they been on your radar, because after the last company—"

"I'm sorry about that, sir, but I do think we should look into buying—"

Now it was my turn to interrupt him. "I want all the information you can give me right after lunch."

"Yes, sir."

"Where are they located?" I didn't want to have to go out of town when I had another business trip in a couple of days.

"San Bernardino, California. If all the data adds up, I think they'd be a perfect fit."

"We'll see. I'll see you after lunch."

"Thank you, sir."

Hanging up, I took a deep breath. I had a feeling I'd be heading out of town sooner than I thought. I had a lot of work to do before Whitmore brought me all the data and I needed coffee.

We had this amazing cinnamon coffee in the employee lounge that I seemed to be addicted to. I knew I could have had my secretary get it for me, but I liked to interact with my employees, and by inter- act, I meant intimidate them. They always worked harder when they saw me walking through the halls. I liked being unpredictable and not one of those bosses no one ever saw.

Color me shocked when I stepped out of my office and saw my secretary actually doing work. I gave her an approving nod and surveyed my surroundings. The moment my eyes made contact with anyone in the halls they looked down and scur- ried away. Perfect.

Opening the door to the lounge, I was shocked to find Pria at the counter typing on her phone. She didn't seem to notice anyone had walked in. I decided to sneak up on her.

Pria continued to type furiously, her mouth turned down in a frown which was so unlike her. Usually, she had a smile that lit up her face. Wrapping my arms around her waist, I nuzzled her neck and rasped out. "Imagine my surprise when I saw you standing here."

Jumping out of my arms, Pria backed away. "What are you doing, Mr. Avery?"

Quirking one eyebrow, I replied while trying to control my dick. Hundreds of women had called me "Mr. Avery" and never had I had such a visceral reaction as I did when Pria said it. "Properly greeting you, Ms. Wang."

With her hands on her hips, she tapped her toe as she looked at me with annoyance. "Do you say hello to all your employees that way? If so, it's only a matter of time until they come down to see *me* and file a grievance against you."

"You're the *only* one I address that way. Pria, what's going on?" This wasn't like her and if Pria had a problem, she had to know she could come to me.

"The problem is, I'm the head of Human Resources and I had sex with my boss."

"I'm very well aware of what we did over the weekend. Did you want a quickie in the copy room because I could probably make that happen?"

"For heaven's sake, no." She closed her eyes and breathed loudly through her nose. When she opened them again, her deep brown irises shone like the lake with a full moon. "Maybe I need to remind you there's a no fraternization policy at Avery Capital Holdings."

"I've heard of it, but it doesn't matter because I'm the owner. Now come over here so I can kiss you."

Her eyes widened with alarm. "You can't be serious? Do you know what would happen if anyone found out about us?" She gave a pregnant pause. "Having sex or that I'm staying at your place?"

"They'd congratulate me?"

"While I like seeing you not being a hard-ass at work, don't do this to me, King. I like you and my job. Don't make me choose."

My brows pulled in as I frowned at her. "You don't have to. You can have both."

"Not if anyone finds out. Please, King. We need to be discreet." Her brown eyes begged me not to make her pick even though she didn't have to.

"If that's what you want then I'll make sure no one sees us in any compromising positions." If Pria thought I wasn't going to spread her out on my desk, she was delusional.

Shaking her head, Pria picked up her cup of coffee as if she was ready to leave. "I can tell that's as far as I'm going to get for now."

"You shouldn't worry." I could be discreet especially knowing how much it meant to her. "How about we meet back at the apartment for a long lunch? We'll take the dogs for a walk and then I'll fuck you on the kitchen counter again."

She licked her lips at the thought. "I'm sorry. I can't today, but how about tomorrow?"

"What do you have going on that you can't meet me?" I didn't like that she was already turning me down for sex. I was addicted to her, and I needed to get my fix, and soon.

"I already have lunch plans. Maybe next time you'll ask me with more advanced notice."

Who the hell was she having lunch with?

"While I've got you, I wanted to talk to you about something. Do you have a few minutes?"

"For you, Ms. Wang, I always have time." Did she see how that worked? I made time for her and she made time for me. "Why don't we go to my office?"

"Thank you, Mr. Avery." Her tone was surprised. Did she think I'd turn her down? "Were you coming for a cup of coffee?" She held up her still steaming cup.

"I was, but you're much better than a caffeine fix."

"You're such a charmer, Mr. Avery." Should I tell her that every time she called me that it made my dick twitch? I wanted to hear her call it out in bed.

"Like I said before, it's all for you, but may I make a recommendation?" She nodded in reply. "Unless you want to suck me off in my office, I suggest you stop calling me Mr. Avery."

"What?" she asked affronted. "I'm not going to call you anything but Mr. Avery at work. It wouldn't seem right."

"I warned you." And I desperately wanted her to continue so I could see her pretty pink lips wrapped around my cock.

"Does anyone else here call you anything but Mr. Avery?" She paused at the door that led out into the hall.

"No, but they also don't affect me the same way you do," I growled out. Was she trying to set a record for how many times she could drive me mad? It was all I could do to remain professional. "Let's go have that meeting now."

Pria looked at me unsure. I was sure she was wondering if I was referring to what she wanted to talk about or what I wanted to do to her. If it was up to me, we'd do both.

I let her walk in front of me by a couple of feet to keep up appearances. I didn't mind though, since I liked watching her ass sway in her tight red skirt.

Even though she was short, her legs looked phenomenal in her sky-high red heels. She didn't pause when we reached my office as she walked right in, and sat down in one of the leather chairs in front of my desk. I guess I'd be hearing her out first.

To give her a bit of the same medicine, she gave me, I directed. "You should have made an appointment with my secretary if you wanted to speak to me."

Her lips thinned as she tapped her finger on the chair arm. "I would have, but you asked, and I only received the email twenty minutes ago."

"Fair enough. What can I help you with?"

"I totally forgot after losing Sarah and then the rest of the events of the weekend, but before all that, I'd taken the dogs to the dog park and met a woman with a goat." That definitely caught my attention, I placed my elbows on my desk and rested my chin on my clasped hands. "We exchanged information about a fundraiser to fight the laws of owning pets in New York. Did you know there are a lot of animals you can't have in the city?"

"Can't say that I do."

"Well, I looked it up and found you pretty much can't have any farm animals. I was surprised at how many you can't have as a pet. I'm not sure how she got away with having a goat here in the city."

"What does this have to do with me?" I wasn't in

the market for having a pet goat or any other animals for that matter.

"She asked if we, and by we, I mean you with a date, and me with a date," she stammered, "would go to the fundraiser. Plus, she needs donations and sponsors and I thought since you love dogs so much maybe you'd like to go."

I wanted to laugh at how she tripped over her words. I couldn't be certain, but I thought it was because she didn't want me to go with anyone else, but I'd told her I didn't do relationships and she was trying to do everything in her power to make it known she didn't think there was an us to be had.

"I'll only go on one condition." I fought the smirk that tried to break free knowing she wouldn't expect my request.

"What's your condition?" she asked in a huff.

"You have to go as my date."

Her eyes widened, and I wanted to laugh. "You want me to be your date? Are you sure that's wise?"

"I don't know. Is it? Will there be other Avery Capital Holdings employees there?" I highly doubted it. It kind of hurt that she wanted to keep what we were doing a secret, but I understood why. Who wanted to be labeled as the boss fucker, especially when there was no chance at a relationship? Only now that I'd spent an entire weekend with only Pria

184

and the dogs, I liked what life looked like with her in my space and in my bed.

"I'm not inviting anyone from here, but I don't have control over the guest list."

"Well, if you want me to go and to donate money, then agree to be my date. It's as simple as that."

"Nothing with you is simple, but I'll agree to go as your date. If we see anyone, we know we can just pretend we bumped into each other."

Ouch. It was like she was ashamed of me. Most women would die to be my date and to be seen on my arm. All but the one woman I wanted there. At least I knew there was no way Pria was using me.

"Whatever makes you feel better."

"Thanks." She smiled sweetly at me before standing. "I should get back to work."

"Are you sure I can't convince you to have lunch with me instead?" I really wanted her to change her mind. Who could she be meeting with that she'd give up an orgasm or two?

Her face softened. "I'm sorry, but I can't cancel. I'll happily see you tonight." Walking around my desk, Pria looked at my closed door before leaning down and brushing her ruby red lips against mine.

"I want you to paint me with those red lips of yours tonight." Preferably my cock, but I kept that to myself.

"I'll see what I can do." She winked before walking out of my office.

✤

FOR THE REST OF THE MORNING, I DID MY OWN DIGGING into Sun Heights Investments. I didn't want to have to go out of town if I didn't have to. Especially when I already had another overnight trip planned at the end of the week. Now that I had a feisty little house-guest, I dreaded going out of town. If I could have brought her with me I would, but there was no reason for it. I had someone I trusted to take care of my dogs.

Since Pria had other plans for lunch, I needed to let the dogs out and put their food in the crockpot since I hadn't done it this morning. I really needed to find someone who could take them for a walk at lunchtime so neither of us had to go home.

After letting my secretary know I was going home for lunch and to expect the information from Whitmore, I headed to the elevator. My steps halted when I saw Pria with a man I knew very well. He had been my family's physician, mostly for my sister, Murphy, and his name was... Mr. Wang. Was he Pria's father? It made sense. They had the same last name and were both Chinese. How had I not figured it out before now?

I thought back to the little girl he would occasionally bring with him. The same little girl who played and hung out with my sister through the years until she went off to college. Had that been Pria? If so, why hadn't she mentioned it to me?

Maybe I had it all wrong and my eyes were deceiving me.

He placed his hand on her lower back and ushered her inside the elevator with a smug smile on his face. Pria, on the other hand, looked anything but happy to be with him. I hung back and watched as the doors closed blocking them from my view.

If Pria had lied about not knowing me and my family, what else had she lied about? In an instant, I decided I was going to check out Sun Heights tonight. I'd still have Whitmore give me the information, but I didn't want to see Pria or listen to her lies right then. If I did, I was sure to say something that I'd regret later. I needed to clear my head and the only way to do that was to be as far away from her as possible.

By the time I got home, I was fuming and sure everything Pria had ever said to me was a lie. Had her fiancé even broke up with her? Was she playing me with pretending she didn't want anyone to find out about us or was it all part of her master plan to seduce me and then sue me for sexual harassment?

Even with Jimmy and Orvy greeting me with lots

of kisses, I was still steaming. I couldn't believe I'd thought Pria was different from all the other women who'd used me in the past when, in fact, she was worse.

I went for a run with Sarah and Orvy to try to clear my head. Maybe I was overreacting, but the second I walked inside my apartment and smelled her scent in every room I went into, I knew my decision to go out of town for the week was the right one. I needed to focus on my business and not what my dick wanted.

I had just finished packing up all the papers I'd printed out from my research and what Whitmore had sent me when I heard the dogs go crazy. That meant only one thing; Pria was here. I could have kicked her out, but I wasn't that much of a dick. At least, not yet. If I found out she really was using me I wouldn't hesitate to slam the door in her face.

Wheeling my suitcase behind me, I strode down the hallway typing on my phone to let my driver know I'd be down in a couple of minutes. Orvy was up on his back legs and his front paws on Pria's shoulders pinning her to the front door as he licked her face. She giggled and hugged him back while Jimmy humped her leg furiously. Maybe he was pissed at her too.

"Down boys," I barked out. Sarah came out of nowhere to see what was going on. Jimmy rushed over and hopped around my legs wanting to be picked up. I scooped him up and scratched behind his ears for a moment before I sat him back down. Orvy bumped my hand with his nose wanting his own scratches so I gave him a few before I patted his head.

Turning back to the liar, I scowled at the sweet smile she had on her face. She really was a talented actress because it looked as if she genuinely cared.

"Hey," she greeted me, going in for a kiss. At the last minute, I turned my head, so she'd get my cheek.

Moving around her, I had my hand on the doorknob when she called my name. I turned to see Pria's brows furrowed as she took in my suitcase. "Where are you going? I thought—"

"What does it matter where I'm going, Ms. Wang? I'm not your boyfriend and I never will be. Watch the dogs while I'm gone." With that, I slammed the door behind me.

19

PRIA

WHAT THE HELL HAD JUST HAPPENED? I CAME BACK TO King's place thinking of all the delicious things we'd do to each other, only for him to sweep past me with a growl and words that hurt deep down in my soul. It didn't make sense and I was determined to find out why King's attitude had taken a complete one-eighty. Even the dogs stood staring at the door wondering why their owner had turned into a dick.

Digging my phone out of my purse, I tried to call King, but after a couple of rings, it went straight to voicemail. I knew that cocky asshole was declining my calls. Unwilling to give up, I called again and again, each time King declining my call until he eventually turned off his phone.

Anger burned deep in my gut as I stewed. Who was he to treat me that way? It was a huge overreaction to not having lunch with him. It didn't matter what he'd said, I couldn't put off seeing my dad another day. It was better to do it willingly than the alternative. He'd been calling and threatening to show up unannounced at work after he found out Haider and I had broken up. He wanted to know what I'd done wrong because, of course, it was my fault things hadn't worked out between us. It was always my fault since I wasn't married and didn't stay at home with two kids on my hip. Once he found out about Haider, my dad hadn't even comforted me. I knew he thought it was my fault for working. I was the black sheep of the family with my modern day thinking. I'd thought about mentioning King to him to only further piss him off, but now I'm glad I hadn't. I would only get another lecture telling me how white men weren't for me and I should only date nice Chinese men. After Haider, and King's earlier attitude, I was thinking I shouldn't date anyone. Fuck men. Me and my vibrator got along just fine.

I wanted to leave his perfect penthouse up in the sky with its perfect views, but I couldn't do that to Jimmy or Orvy. One thing I knew was I needed to find my own place and fast. Whenever King came back, I would be leaving.

He hadn't even mentioned how long he'd be gone. I decided to call his secretary saying I needed to make an appointment at Mr. Avery's earliest convenience.

"Mr. Avery's office this is Mandy speaking. How can I help you?" she answered with an annoyed huff. I wasn't sure how she still had her job. If I didn't know better, I would have thought King was fucking her and that was why he was keeping her around. Maybe he was and his speech was all a big lie.

"Hi, Mandy. This is Pria Wang and I need to make an appointment with Mr. Avery as soon as possible."

"I don't know why. You just had a meeting with him this morning," she muttered, not intending for me to hear her. "Let me look and see when his next available time is." She hummed as if she was checking but I wasn't sure if she actually was or if she was just wasting my time. "I can get you in on Tuesday next week at ten if that works for you."

"He doesn't have anything sooner?" I knew he was busy, but that was a long time. "I only need a few minutes. If you could just let—"

"I'm sorry but that's the earliest I can get you in. Mr. Avery is out of the office for the rest of the week and he has meetings all day on Monday. If anyone cancels, I can contact you to see if that time will work for you."

I wasn't sure what to do. I didn't need to make an appointment with him, but I also wasn't sure if King would talk to me once he got home. Plus, I planned to be out of here the moment he stepped foot in his apartment. He said no matter what happened between us, I'd keep my job, but I wanted to remind him of that fact.

"Yes, please put me down for Tuesday and if anything opens up reschedule my appointment."

"Sure thing, Ms. Wang," she snipped before hanging up.

If things were better between King and me, I'd try to talk him into firing her. She was the worst secretary on the planet. Laying down on the couch the dogs jumped up with me. One cuddled me on each side like they were giving me a sweet hug. I was going to miss them when I left.

Orvy placed his head on my arm and looked up at me. His eyes looked sad as if he knew what was going on. "Why is your daddy being such an asshole?" Orvy's only response was to lift his head and place it a little closer to my shoulder. God, he was so sweet. Even Jimmy wasn't humping me. Luckily, he only seemed to try and hump me when one foot was on the ground. He was such a strange but lovable little dog.

It was unbelievable that earlier in the day, I'd wanted to slowly peel King's expensive suit off his body and trace every inch of his skin with my mouth and hands, and now I wanted to take scissors to every suit in his closet before I ripped off his balls.

With the dogs snuggled up to me, and my body warmed, I started to relax. My eyelids started to droop and thoughts of my asshole boss slowly drifted away.

I woke with a start. Haider's ringtone blared in the quiet of the room causing me to bolt upright. Jimmy and Orvy grumbled beside me as I hit the power button to silence the offending noise. I didn't want to talk to him now or ever. There was nothing he could possibly need to say to me. The only person I wanted to talk to didn't seem to want to talk to me. Now that I'd slept some, I'd calmed down and was only more bewildered by his swift change of behavior.

After serving the dogs their dinner, I picked up my phone and tried to call King again but it went straight to voicemail. It had been hours and I hoped with some time he'd realized he'd overreacted and was ready to talk. It baffled my mind what could have set him off. I'd agreed to be his date even against my better judgment. I didn't want to think of what would happen if anyone found out about us or what we'd done. King's thought on how the no frat-ernization policy didn't apply to him because he was the boss was so like him. Nothing seemed to faze him, but he needed to understand, just because no one would think much about him fucking an employee, I wouldn't be taken seriously. How could I enforce the same policy I was defying?

The smell of his cologne permeated the place almost making me dizzy. It was intoxicating and heartbreaking now that he wasn't there. How had I let him wedge himself so far into my heart in such a short amount of time? Everywhere I looked I could see him smiling down at his dogs or wrapping his arms around me and nuzzling into my neck. Deciding I needed to get out of his space, I grabbed the dogs' leashes. We were going to go for a nice long walk and maybe even pick up some food on the way back. The cool fall air would hopefully do wonders for my mood and maybe give me some clarity on the events of the day.

The dogs wagged their little and big butts by the door as I hooked their leashes on. Even Sarah was excited to go out with us. Hopefully, she wouldn't make me regret my decision to bring her along.

The sun had set an hour ago making the air cooler than it had been during the day. I zipped my sweatshirt up to keep the chill at bay. Of course, the dogs didn't seem to notice, and I doubted they would until it was winter. I headed in the direction of the dog park even though we weren't going there. I wasn't sure of the hours, but it was probably closed.

I quickly figured out there was no way in hell I was

going to be able to get any food with three dogs in tow. It wasn't to say places weren't friendly because they were. It was all because I had two giant dogs that could pull me this way and that without any trouble at all. If I wanted something to eat, I'd get it after I took the dogs home. They'd be fine without me and I liked the idea of being away from King's place. I wasn't sure where I'd go, but the longer I thought about it the more I liked the idea. I picked up my pace as we made our way back to their home. I had to remind myself it wasn't mine. It was a temporary residence I would soon leave.

Unclipping the dogs from their leashes, I hung them up and looked down at my clothes before deciding to stay in what I had on. I'd changed into yoga pants, a T-shirt, a sweatshirt over it, and a pair of tennis shoes for their walk since there was no way in hell I could walk in heels and a skirt with them. Grabbing my purse, I gave each of the dogs a pat on the head before I headed out.

I felt lighter the moment I stepped out of the building. All thoughts of King, Haider, and my dad were long gone. I slipped my earbuds in and pulled up Spotify. I hit whatever the daily mix was and set out in the opposite direction than I'd taken the dogs. There weren't many food places in that direction, which was why I always walked that way with the three amigos.

One thing King's area didn't have was an abundance of trees. I missed seeing all the leaves changing color in the fall. I knew all I had to do was head to Central Park to get my fill, but I missed it, nonetheless.

My head swiveled back and forth as I took in everything around me. I wasn't accustomed to the area and didn't really know what was around. When King had been home, he ordered out every night. I wasn't sure what I was in the mood for, only that I'd know when I saw or smelled it. The only thing I knew I didn't want was Chinese food. I wasn't sure if I'd ever eat it again with how much it had been crammed down my throat first by my family and then Haider. Didn't they know variety was the spice of life?

A hard push from behind sent me into a quiet side street that was full of trash and smelled like piss. Whirling around I was caught short by a hand to my throat and rank breath wafting over my face.

"Give me your purse and you won't get hurt," a deep and snarling voice said hidden behind a dark hood.

There was no way to know if I gave him my purse, he would let me go. In that moment, I wished I knew some sort of self-defense, but my dad had never let me do any extracurricular activities but play the piano and the violin. Neither would help me now.

Still, I had to do something. If this guy was willing to steal from me who was to say he wasn't willing to go further. He could rape or kill me.

Throwing all of my one hundred and ten pounds into his hulking frame I tried to get away. I must have shocked him because he stumbled back a few steps. I thought I'd make the short distance out of the quiet street until he grabbed the back of my sweatshirt. When it ripped, I still thought I might get away until he grabbed my arm and pulled it back at a jarring angle. Pain shot through me, but I continued to fight for my life. I scratched down his arm with my other hand; I was about to scream for help like I should have done the moment he trapped me in the alley when he punched me in the eye. The hit sent shockwaves through my head and neck as I saw stars. A guttural moan came out as I clutched my eye with my other hand. I'd never once even been slapped in my entire life let alone been hit. The pain felt like a shot of blinding fire through my eye socket, causing me to stagger back into the wall.

"You shouldn't have done that, bitch. If you only would have cooperated…" He ripped my purse from my shoulder. I was amazed it had stayed in place and not fallen to the ground. He towered over me as one hand pinned my hands above my head and the other went to the waistband of my yoga pants and slipped his hand inside. Agonizing pain shot down my arm, but I fought through it. I had no other choice.

No.

No.

No.

I would rather die than have this man rape me. When two fingers slipped into my panties my entire body started to shake and I knew I had to act. Lifting one knee, I rammed it into his groin as hard as I could, but it didn't seem to affect him at all. My only chance and I'd ruined it.

"You fucking bitch," he howled. Rearing back his arm, he let it fly. I tried to block it to no avail. His fist slammed into my temple and I went down. My vision started to go black as he sat on top of me and continued to pound into my face and stomach.

The last thing I remembered before everything went black was someone yelling. It sounded so far away, I only hoped they got to me before he raped or killed me.

GROGGILY, I WOKE UP TO MACHINES BEEPING AND THE smell of antiseptic. I tried to turn over on my side but stopped as pain ricocheted through my upper body. I let out a low groan and attempted to bring my hands to my face when I felt a tug and pinch in my left hand. Cracking my eyes open, I examined my surroundings. White ceilings and walls surrounded me. I looked down at my hand and saw an IV attached. I was definitely in the hospital. I wasn't sure how I'd gotten there. Before I passed out from the pain and injury, I'd heard someone, but that was all I remembered.

"Hey, honey," a soft voice said from the other side of the room. "You're finally awake."

Finally? How long had I been out?

"You've been here for…" she looked down at her watch. "A little over an hour, give or take. I'm glad to see you're awake. I'll get the doctor in here to talk to you and we'll get you some pain meds. You've got to be hurting."

I tried to nod, but it hurt too much. I would very much like something to take away the pain. "That would be wonderful."

"I'll be back in a few minutes, honey. Don't worry. You'll be feeling right as rain soon enough."

I wasn't so sure about that.

After about ten minutes, a man in his late fifties walked in with a kind smile on his face. His hair was completely gray, but he was good-looking for his age.

"Can you tell me your name?"

"Pria Wang." That was easy.

He asked a series of questions that I answered. "Can you tell me what happened to you tonight?"

Not so easy. "I was mugged, and I fought back. He..." I gulped at what he'd tried to do. I hoped he wasn't successful. "I think he wanted to rape me. I blacked out when he had me pinned to the ground. Did he..."

"We'll have to do a rape kit to be one hundred percent sure since you were unconscious. We're waiting for CT to open up and we'll get you scanned before we put a cast on your arm. Besides a broken arm, you have multiple contusions to your face and some bruised ribs. It may not seem like it but you're very lucky."

Lucky. It sure didn't feel like it.

"It will probably be another twenty to thirty minutes before someone will come in to take you down. I'll have the nurse bring you some pain meds before you're moved. Is there anyone that you'd like us to call for you?" He wrote something in his chart while he continued to smile kindly at me.

"Is my sweatshirt here? I had my phone in it."

The nurse who I hadn't noticed was still in the room went over to a bag that sat in the corner of the room and fished out my sweatshirt. I closed my eyes praying my phone was still inside my zip up pocket. She patted around and then smiled when she hit something. "Looks like you were lucky. He didn't steal your phone."

I couldn't imagine all the people who came

through their doors after being mugged and even worse. Even though I didn't think I was lucky, they did, and I'd take their word on it.

She brought my phone to me and patted my hand. "If you need anything all you have to do is hit the red button. I'll be back in a few minutes with some medicine that will make you feel better."

"Thanks," I responded looking down at my phone. Not one missed call or text. I didn't want to call and have to deal with my dad, but I knew I needed to somehow get in contact with King.

Not knowing when I'd be able to leave, I sent an email to King's secretary letting her know that he needed to find someone else to take the dogs out in the morning and probably for the rest of the day since I was in the hospital. I hoped I'd be released sometime tomorrow. I hated hospitals. I'd spent too much time in one when my mom had cancer. The only thing I knew as I waited for my CT was that *everything* hurt, and my arm was broken. Even if I got out the next day there would be no way I could walk the dogs unless it was one at a time and probably not even then.

Fuck my life.

20

KINGSTON

TAPPING THE TOE OF MY LEATHER SHOE, I WAITED IN THE VIP lounge for my flight to be called. When I headed for the airport, I had no idea how long I would have to wait. Now I was regretting not waiting until the next day. I'd blocked Pria's phone calls after the fifth time she called, and to get my mind off her, I decided to start answering emails. I'd been so distracted throughout the day, I'd barely gotten any work done.

My phone pinged with another email. It was a never-ending cycle of emails that came in day and night. If my secretary was even remotely competent, I would have had her answering some of them, but I didn't trust her, so I had to answer all of them. Some days it felt like all I did was answer email after email. After this week, I needed to find a new secretary. If I wasn't pissed at Pria, I would have asked her to find me the perfect secretary. I finished responding to Whitmore, letting him know I would be meeting someone at Sun Heights tomorrow and hit send. Looking at my emails I saw the latest one that had come in was flagged by my secretary. I knew it was important if she flagged it since she'd yet to do so.

She'd forwarded me an email from Pria stating I needed to find someone else to take care of the dogs tonight and tomorrow. What the fuck! I thought I could trust her to stay with them and they'd be safe. I continued reading only to drop my phone when it said she was in the hospital. What had happened?

I emailed Cindy or Sandy or whatever her name was and had her email Pria back to ask what hospital she was at and to text me the name of the hospital as soon as she found out. Her time was short at the company. While she had flagged the email, it would have been prudent for her to call me to make sure I knew about Pria and the dogs. I could have been in California by the time I saw the email and too far away to be of any help. Once I hit send, I popped up from my seat and made my way out front to where the taxis waited. I only hoped there was one available. I didn't want to have to wait for an Uber. Luck wasn't on my side. I wasn't sure how there were no taxis out front at JFK, but it was like God was pissed at me for leaving without talking to Pria.

My phone beeped with a text from Sandy letting me know Pria was at Mount Sinai. For a moment I felt bad that I'd never learned her name and thought I should learn it, but did I really need to if I was going to replace her as soon as I possibly could?

I ordered an Uber and hated that it would take me almost an hour to get to Pria. Had Sarah pulled her down again? The email hadn't mentioned anything being wrong with any of the dogs. I called the front desk at my building and asked for someone to check on the dogs and to make sure they were okay. I could hear the confusion in George's tone, but he assured me they'd be checked on.

No matter how hard I tried to work as my driver and I made our way from the airport to the hospital, I couldn't stop thinking about Pria. Maybe she twisted her ankle while out on a walk. It couldn't be serious. It didn't matter how mad I was at Pria for lying to me, I wanted to check on her to make sure she was okay. I ended up staring out at the city as we made our way to the hospital.

Once the hospital came into view, I had my briefcase in hand and was ready to jump out of the car. Luckily, I hadn't checked my suitcase, otherwise, it would be on its way to California right now instead of sitting beside me.

The moment the car stopped, I was out of the car

and on a mission to find Pria. Luckily, I found someone who could help me. She was scowling at her computer screen when I approached.

"Excuse me could you tell me where I can find Pria Wang? I was informed she checked in earlier tonight."

Her dark eyes flicked up to me and then back down to her screen as she typed furiously. "She's still in the emergency room."

"Can you tell me which room?" Hearing she was in the ER worried me, but where else would she be?

"It says only family is allowed back. Are you her—"

"I'm her fiancé." The words came out before I could stop them, but it didn't matter. I'd make up any lie for a chance to see her.

"She's in twelve-C."

I scanned the area for a sign to point me in the right direction. Hospitals weren't new to me, but I didn't know my way around this one. The only thing I knew was that the emergency room was on the first floor. I didn't have to find the right elevator to make my way upstairs.

Turning left and right, and then right and left, I finally saw the entrance to the emergency room and breathed a sigh of relief. I trained my eyes on the room numbers. With each moan and cry from the rooms I passed, my mind got away from me. It didn't matter that I was mad at Pria. I only wanted her to be okay. There were so many people in the ER and the smell of urine, vomit, and antiseptic brought back unwanted memories of Murphy.

Finally, after seemingly circling the entire emergency room twice, I found 12-C. The door was closed and now that I was there, I was unsure of what to do. I had been a total dick earlier when I left leaving Pria confused and probably not wanting anything to do with me ever again. I decided not to knock. I didn't want her to know it was me and turn me away. Instead, I quietly slipped inside. I was happy to see she was in a room and not one of the beds with only a curtain around it.

Pria lay on the bed staring up at the ceiling and even from the doorway I could see the tears slipping down her bruised and battered cheek. Her entire face was swollen with cuts and bruises marring its usual perfection. There was no way the dogs did this unless they dragged her out in front of a car. One black casted arm rested on her stomach as the other brushed away her tears.

"Pria," I gasped, rushing toward her. "Oh my God, what happened?" I didn't wait for her to answer. As delicately as I could, I pulled her into my arms and buried my face in her hair. Her good arm wrapped around me as she buried her face in my chest and started to sob. "I'm so sorry," I whispered repeatedly into the top of her head. If I'd stayed and talked to her none of this would have happened. The guilt almost brought me to my knees.

When her sobs calmed, I pulled back to look at her. One eye was swollen shut, and the other was red and puffy from crying with a gash above her eyebrow. My fingers itched to wipe away her tears only I was too afraid I'd hurt her. "What happened?"

She sucked in a hitched breath. Her eyes welled again with tears that were about to spill over with only a blink of the eye. "I… I was so mad at you that I did-didn't want to be in your space. Your sm-smell was everywhere." She hiccupped and then grimaced. Her casted arm held her ribs.

"I can't express to you how sorry I am. I'll do anything for you to forgive me." I kissed her forehead and stroked her hair back from her face.

"You didn't do this to me. I was mugged and…"

There was more? Had she been…

"Were you raped?" I choked out. I would never be able to live with myself if she was.

"I don't know. He tried, but I fought back and that's when he started hitting me. I woke up here, so I don't know what happened after I was unconscious."

No, not my little Pria. She didn't deserve this.

"Someone is supposed to come and do a rape kit, but I don't know when." She rested the side of her face against my shoulder. "I'm still waiting to hear about my CT scan."

"Fucking hell, Pria. I'm so sorry. From now on you use my driver. He'll be at your beck and call."

Separating from me, she looked up at me as her eyes searched for something. "How are you even here? Your secretary said you were out of town for the rest of the week. When I emailed her to find someone to watch the dogs, I didn't expect you to show up here. I only wanted someone to take care of Jimmy, Orvy, and Sarah."

"I was still at the airport when I got the email and once I found out you were in the hospital, I had to make sure you were okay. I know I was pissed earlier, but—"

"Ms. Wang," a voice interrupted. Turning to the door, a sweet older looking nurse stood inside the door. "I'm here to do your rape kit. I was told you're unsure if you were raped or not.

I looked down at Pria with what could only be horror in my eyes. It was possible someone had violated her because I was an asshole.

Pria bit down on her split lip and winced. "I don't think he did, but I can't be sure. I'm sore everywhere and…"

"That's all right. Say no more. I'll explain to you

what will be done, and you can decide if you want to continue. It's your right to have one just as it's your right to deny it. If your…"

"Fiancé," I added. Pria's gaze shifted to mine. It looked as if she was about to deny my claim, so I whispered to her, "I'll explain later."

"If he can sit in the waiting room, I'll have someone come get him when we're done." She smiled kindly.

"I can't stay?" I clasped Pria's hand in mine. "Do you want me here?"

"Sir, I think it would be best if you weren't in the room. It can be invasive, and many women find having their significant other in the room more difficult. We don't want that, do we?"

Of course, I didn't want to make it worse for Pria. I only wished none of this had happened. "Will she be released afterward?"

The nurse flipped open the chart in her hand and scanned through the information. "That will depend on what the CT scan shows and what the doctor on call determines."

Leaning down, I pressed a light kiss to the top of Pria's head. It was hard to find a place that didn't look like my touch would cause her pain. "I'll be waiting for you in the waiting room."

"You don't need to do that, King."

"I do so don't argue with me." I gave her hand a final squeeze before I set out to find the waiting room. It wasn't hard, but it wasn't where I wanted to be. No one had directed me to any other waiting room, so I was stuck out with everyone who was waiting their turn to be seen.

Trying to block out the people around me and the memories of the many times Murphy had been rushed to the emergency room, I sent off an email to my secretary letting her know to cancel my hotel reservations, flights, and meetings for the week. The email took me no time at all and before I knew it my mind had slipped into the past.

MY ONCE BEAUTIFUL SISTER WAS FAILING. SHE WAS A sliver of her past self. Her lungs were giving out and I couldn't remember the last time she ate solid food. I held her hand as I sat by the side of her bed with my head resting next to her arm. She'd been admitted thirty-six hours ago, and had been in and out of sleep unlike me, who couldn't sleep no matter how hard I tried. And I wanted to sleep. I wanted to wake up from this nightmare and have my healthy sister back because I knew... I knew this was the end. No matter what medicines she was given or exper-imental treatments, nothing worked, and we had to watch her waste away into the fragile girl who lay before me.

A light squeeze to my hand had me looking up to see Murphy's eyes open and alert. "Hey, your majesty. What are you doing here? Shouldn't you be at work or on a date?"

Murphy thought it was funny my friends in grade school started to call me King. In turn, she liked to pretend I was some royal asshole. I was an asshole, but never to her. Not one day in all of her existence had I ever said or done anything that wasn't loving. She didn't deserve to be sick and I hated her disease for slowly taking her away from me.

"By your side is the only place I ever want to be, Murph." I felt tears sting the backs of my eyes, but I fought them back. I didn't want to upset her. I didn't want her to lose hope.

A shaky smile spread across her face. "You're going to have to take care of my dogs." I groaned playfully. "I know they can be a handful, but I love them."

I knew she did. Murphy spoiled those dogs worse than any grandparent spoiled their grandkid.

"I'm sorry, Kingston." It was so quiet I almost missed it. I was shocked to find tears brimming in her eyes when I looked up.

"You have nothing to be sorry for. You're the best sister anyone could ask for." I choked out each word since they wanted to come out as a sob, but I swore to myself I would be strong for her. She'd been so strong all her life. Even then as she wasted away in a hospital bed.

"I'll love you forever and ever, big brother." Her smile turned watery. *Simultaneously, a tear slipped down both our cheeks.*

"As I'll love you forever and ever for all eternity."

After that Murphy insisted that I go and check on her dogs. She didn't want them to be alone since she hadn't been able to spend much time with them lately. On my way back to the hospital, my mother called me in hysterics, and I knew without her saying a word my sister was gone.

"MR. AVERY." THE NURSE FROM EARLIER STOOD BEFORE me with the same kind smile on her face. "I'm finished with Ms. Wang. She'd like you to join her again. If you'll follow me, I'll escort you back to her room."

I stood quickly. Murphy was still on my mind and I didn't want to be there. The memory of the last time I'd been in a hospital was still fresh, and it made me think of all the things that could have happened to Pria. Of how much worse it could have been. I followed behind the nurse as she expertly made her way back to Pria's room. She patted me on the arm once we got there.

"Hang in there, young man."

I thought it was strange for her to be telling me that, but I didn't care. It was unusual to have all these feelings bubbling around. It was as if a well of emotions had erupted inside of me when I read Pria was in the hospital. My heart stopped and then started beating double time when I realized how important she was to me.

When I walked in, Pria's closed eyes fluttered open when she heard me. I made my way over to the bed and clasped her hand in mine. She looked so tiny in her hospital bed. All I wanted to do was get her out of there and take her home.

"Hey, are you okay?" Pria asked softly.

"Shouldn't I be asking you that question?" I smiled thinly down at her.

Her tiny hand brushed against my cheek and her finger came away with moisture. I hadn't realized that a tear had escaped until then.

"What's going on with you today? I've got to say you're giving me whiplash and that's not good in my condition."

She probably thought I was a basket case with the way I'd acted. First, wanting to spend my lunch between her legs to raging at her when she got home only now for me to be crying.

"I'm sorry about today. About everything. I was an asshole, which isn't news, but if it wasn't for me leaving, you wouldn't be here." I laced my fingers through hers and tried to smile, but I knew I wasn't successful. Guilt was going to be on the menu for a long time to come. Every time I looked at her it reminded me that if I'd bothered to stay to talk to her, Pria wouldn't have been trying to escape all things, *me*.

"You can't know that." She shrugged and winced. "I'm fine. They've given me some good drugs, so don't feel guilty. We could have talked, and I could have stormed out and the same thing could have happened."

"That doesn't make me feel better. I seem to be the common denominator for the reason why you're leaving and getting hurt." I sat down in the chair beside the bed, keeping her hand in mine the entire time. "Let me feel guilty. It's my penance."

"If it makes you feel better the nurse said I wasn't raped." Her bottom lip started to tremble on the last word, and I wanted to kick my own ass. I needed to be here for Pria and keep my guilt to myself.

Nodding my head, I rubbed my thumb over the back of her arm. "I'm glad you don't have to go through that as well, but it wouldn't have changed the way I see you."

"And how do you see me?" she asked on a shaky breath.

I held nothing back telling her the absolute truth of my feelings for her. "Strong, resilient, feisty, smart, kind and caring, beyond gorgeous, and my perfect match. You were made for me. No one else besides my family has ever made me want to show them who I really am." I hung my head, unable to look her in the eye.

"I like what you show me, King," She spoke softly but with conviction in her voice. With those simple but profound words, I knew she was being honest with me. "When we met in your office all I could think was you were a cocky suit, well, besides the obvious." I tilted my head looking at her through the hair that hung over my eyes. Lightheartedness filled her voice. "Don't make me feed your ego. You know you're gorgeous. Your only flaw is being an asshole."

"I have a few more, but yeah, being a cocky asshole is a good way to keep people away. Most don't want to put up with me, but you... you've got me by the balls."

Pria closed her eyes for a long moment. I thought she'd fallen asleep from the drugs until she blew out a long breath. With her eyes still closed, she asked, "Want to tell me what earlier was all about?"

"None of that matters now. Only that you're going to be okay and you don't hate me." I paused thinking that Pria had never said she wasn't still mad at me. "Do you hate me?"

Her good eye slit open. "If I hated you, I wouldn't have had the nurse bring you back." She closed her eyes again. "Now, tell me what happened. Did I do something? Is it because we didn't have lunchtime sex?"

It hurt that she would even think that about me, but I knew I hadn't given her any clues as to why I'd been furious with her.

"I saw you on my way to lunch with..." I gritted my teeth because it still stung to know she'd lied to me. "I saw you with your dad and when I did it all clicked. Well, not all, but I knew who you were then. Why didn't you say we knew each other? You had ample opportunity to tell me you knew me and my sister."

Pria let out a puff of air. "At first, it was because you didn't recognize me. I know I'm not memorable, but still, I thought you'd know who I was. After that, I didn't think it would matter since I didn't think we'd have much contact. What did it matter if my dad was your family physician and I used to hang out with your sister? I even babysat you a couple of times."

It made sense as to why she hadn't mentioned it then especially if we were only going to be acquaintances.

"The next time I had the opportunity was when you said Murphy had named your dogs. I was going to say something then, but you stormed off. After that, it never seemed like the right moment. I wanted to tell you, but you're one hell of a distraction. I'm sorry I didn't tell you and you had to find out the way you did."

Lacing our fingers together, I brought her hand up and placed a soft kiss to the back of it. "I'm sorry I didn't recognize you. If I had, then maybe none of this would have happened."

"When you saw us, you should have come up to us and said something." A small smile pulled at the corner of her lips.

"What's that look for?" I asked with my own smile. Even after all the shit of the day, she could still manage to make me smile and that was everything.

"I was imagining you telling my dad we're fucking and the look on his face. He probably would have imploded on the spot."

"Why?" My brows creased. "I'm a perfectly acceptable male specimen."

She giggled and then clutched at her side. "Please don't make me laugh. It hurts too much. But really is that how you see yourself as an acceptable male specimen?" She shook her head at me. "You're anything but acceptable."

"Then what am I?" I was starting to get worried she thought even less of me.

"You are prime grade A beef. A father should strive for their daughters to meet a man like you."

"So your dad would be happy?" It didn't make sense.

"Just the opposite. He's old school and thinks I should only be with a good Chinese man. He thinks Haider cheating on me was all my doing. He'd be absolutely appalled I'm with a white man."

It was shocking to know he thought that way. What I wanted to know was did Pria feel the same way. Was she only with me to defy her father?

"What are your thoughts on being with an insanely wealthy white man with blond hair and green eyes who's devilishly handsome and hung like a horse?"

"There he is. My cocky asshole." Her words may have been harsh, but she looked at me with love in her eyes, or at least I thought it looked something like love.

"Right here. Now, what are your thoughts? I want to know," I demanded but kept my tone light.

She tightened her grip on my hand and motioned for me to come closer. I didn't stop until there was only an inch between our noses. "If it was anyone but you, I wouldn't want him. I like you for *you*, King. I don't care what you look like or the size of your dick. That may have been what attracted me to you in the beginning, but it was you, the man buried deep inside that only me and your trio of dogs get to see that kept me by your side."

And at that moment, I knew I was in love with Pria Wang. If she hadn't been in a hospital bed. If we had been anywhere else, I would have dropped down on one knee and proposed to her after hearing those words.

Instead, I had to wait.

21

PRIA

Since the attack, I'd only been back at the office for two days. King had demanded that I stay home and rest. At first, I thought it would only be a few days, but once I was discharged and realized how much every motion I made elicited a great deal of pain, I ended up working from his place. My options were to work and feel pain or take the drugs they'd prescribed for me and be a loopy mess since nothing else seemed to work.

King had been out of town for the last four days on the business trips he'd canceled to be with me when he found out I was in the hospital. When he walked into the room in the ER, I was shocked. I was ready to write him off after he'd left his apartment, but after our talk, I was one hundred and ten percent in love with him. He'd called and FaceTimed me every night he was gone, making sure I was okay and that the new dog walker was treating the dogs well. There was no way I was going to be walking any of them except Jimmy in the near future. It was too easy for either Sarah or Orvy to jerk me around and I wanted my ribs to heal as quickly as possible.

My phone vibrated with an incoming call. Warmth flowed through my body and settled in my chest when I saw it was King calling.

"Hey, what are you doing calling me?" I looked at the clock on my wall that read six forty-five. "I thought you'd be in a meeting right about now."

"I'm getting ready to head inside in just a minute, but I wanted to say hi. Are you still at work?"

I knew I should have already left, but I'd been busy dealing with one employee who went off on a tirade during a meeting, and another who had harassed a fellow employee about her period. Getting the statements from everyone who'd been at the meeting had taken most of the day, which is why I was still there even after the sun had started to go down.

"I am, but I was just getting ready to pack up and leave after I called your driver to let him know I was ready."

"Good girl." I could hear the smile in his voice. "Before you go, can you pick up a package in my office for me?"

"Sure." I wasn't sure why he wanted me to get it

when he could pick it up tomorrow when he got in, but I didn't argue.

"It's something for you and I want you to have it right away." He must have heard the uncertainty in my voice about retrieving his package.

"Ah, you didn't have to do that, King, but that's very sweet of you." I packed up my stuff a little quicker so I could see what he'd gotten me.

"Wait until you see what it is." The husky tone in his voice caught me off guard. Had he gotten me some lingerie to wear once he was back? King may have said he was used to pleasuring himself, but I felt the hard-on he woke with every morning. While I was sure he'd seen to himself while he was gone, I knew he wanted the real thing. It got me hot and bothered thinking of him touching himself.

"You've got me intrigued, Mr. Avery. I can't wait to see what you got me. I'm leaving my office now. Do you want to stay on the phone with me while I open it?" I felt like a giddy schoolgirl about ready to open all her presents on Christmas Day. I couldn't remember the last time someone got me something for the hell of it.

"I'd love nothing more."

The amusement in his tone halted me in my tracks. "Is this a prank?"

"No, Pria, it most certainly is not a prank. Go see

what I got for you. I think you'll be happy with what you find."

"I hope your secretary isn't at her desk, because it could get awkward. If you could have seen the look on her face yesterday when she saw me. I don't know why she hates me so much." If she could have killed me with the daggers from her eyes, she would have, and it made no sense why she hated me. I'd never done anything to her except expect her to do her job.

"You need to start looking for her replacement. She's the worst secretary I've ever had." He sighed heavily. "I shouldn't have fired my previous one for letting you in to see me with my pants down."

"Who knows what would have happened if I hadn't seen you tucking yourself in that day?"

King hummed down the line. "I knew you were only with me for my cock."

"It is mighty in every way."

I slowed my steps as I came closer to King's office. I wasn't sure how I'd get in if Mandy was at her desk, but with King being gone I didn't see her staying past five.

"It doesn't look like she's here. I'm going in," I whispered to King.

"Why are you whispering?" he asked, whispering back.

"Because I don't want to be caught."

"I'm giving you permission if anyone asks."

"Thanks, but I don't want to explain why you asked me to pick something up in your office after hours."

I quickly snuck into King's office and shut the door behind me. It was dark inside, but I didn't want to turn on the lights and let anyone know I was inside.

"Hang on. Let me put you on speaker. It's dark in here and I need to use my phone's flashlight to see. Are you sure she put the package in here? It could be at her desk."

"I'm one hundred percent positive it's in my office." The voice came from behind me and I nearly screamed. Twirling around, I threw myself at the man standing in front of me. He caught me gently around the waist thinking about my injuries more than I had. Picking me up with one arm wrapped around my back and the other under my ass, he brought me to his mouth and kissed me with tenderness.

"King," I gasped against his lips when we broke apart, "what are you doing here?"

"Surprising you. Hopefully, it was a good one?"

"The best one. Never in a million years would I have guessed *you* were my present."

"I wish I could have seen your face better." King peppered kisses over my eyes, nose, and cheeks.

"Why didn't you just surprise me at your place?"

"I thought we could live out one of my fantasies. I know I can't bend you across my desk or get too physical, but I've been dying to sink into your heat since the first time you stepped foot in here. What do you say about helping me out?"

"I say I think I should reward you for surprising me."

Before the last word was out of my mouth, King started to move first to lock the door and then over to the couch he had in his office. Luckily, he always kept his blinds closed, so we didn't have to worry about that. If we got caught... I didn't want to think about it.

King sat down and slid his other hand down to the hem of my skirt. My legs were on either side of his. I kneeled on the couch and let him push my skirt above my waist. "Hold on tight," he murmured right before he ripped my thong off.

My mouth crashed into his and our tongues dueled. His need for me was incredibly hot and spurred me on.

Now bare, I started to rub back and forth against the bulge that was fighting to break through his suit pants. I didn't care that I'd leave a mark all over his fly. My only thought was that I wanted to feel him against me. My fingers started to undo the buttons of his shirt. It was dark, but the city lights illuminated his office enough to let me see the contours of his torso the farther down I went. I wished I could have ripped it off like he'd done my panties.

"I want to feel you skin to skin." My ribs were still tender and I'd been wearing button-up blouses so I didn't have to lift my arms above my head. King was much quicker at removing mine than I was his. Pulling one cup down, he took my breast into his mouth. His tongue swirled around my pebbled nipple in delicious swipes. Moaning, I rocked into him harder, rubbing my clit against his zipper for friction, but it wasn't enough.

My hands ran down the soft skin over hard muscle until I came into contact with his belt. Quickly, I undid it, had his zipper down, and was pulling his hot length out and wrapped my hand around his steel shaft. Placing it at my entrance, I slowly sank down until I took every inch of him inside. When he finally bottomed out, we both moaned.

"You feel so fucking good. I've been dreaming about your sweet little pussy and what it would feel like to be inside of you again. Nothing compares." He groaned. The deep sound filled the room.

With both hands on my hips, King slowly withdrew and pumped up again and again. Even though he was frenzied before, he still took care of me and made sure not to hurt me. His movements were slow, as were his kisses as he took my mouth. It felt different than anything we'd ever done before. This time it was with our professed feelings between us. In his office with us on his couch, King made love to me. Each slow glide in and out felt like heaven.

As slowly as we moved together, my pleasure came at a record pace and going by King's sounds and strained movements, I'd say his did the same. My hips rocked a little faster as King's thumb found my clit and rubbed it in slow, small circles.

Our mouths broke apart as my back arched and heat licked up my spine. Stars blurred my vision as the most intense jolt of pleasure shot through my body. I felt electrified as I tensed and then sagged into King's embrace. His grip on me tightened as he held himself deep within me for a long moment.

Panting into his neck, I smiled. "That was the best surprise ever."

A noise came from outside that sounded like someone had run into a wall and had me sitting up straight. "What was that?" I whispered. If anyone had been out there, it was too late to be quiet now.

"I think you're hearing things. What do you say we go out to eat before we head home? Whatever you're in the mood for."

"Like a date?" I tried to see the look on his face, but it was covered in shadow.

One hand slid up my spine and cupped the nape of my neck. "Yes, Pria. Would you go on a date with me tonight?" The tone in his voice was something I'd never heard from him. It was unsure, and I wanted to remove any hesitance from him ever again.

"Why, Mr. Avery, I thought you'd never ask?" In all truth, I never thought we'd go anywhere in public. Before I thought I was just a convenient lay and now I had no clue what to expect from King. He was a surprisingly sweet man when he wanted to be.

"All in good time, my dear. Now let's get dressed so I can feed you. I have a plan to keep you up late into the night and you'll need your strength."

I liked the sound of that.

We dressed quickly in the dark. I wasn't happy I had to go out with no underwear on while wearing a skirt, but I didn't have a choice. It made me hot all over again thinking about how King ripped them off me.

Stepping outside his office a tall, dark, and handsome man stood by the desk with a quizzical look on his face. He turned toward us when he heard us coming out of the office.

"Graham, what are you doing here? I didn't forget a meeting or anything did I?" King shook his hand with a boyish smile on his face.

"Nope, I came by to see if you wanted to get dinner." His friend looked me up and down assessing me. "I don't mean to be rude, but were you doing a threesome and piss the other girl off?"

What!

King and I turned to look at each other with confused faces. His brows and lips turned down. "What the hell are you talking about? This is Pria, my..." My breathing stopped as I waited for King's next words. "She's my girlfriend and we're not into that sort of thing."

"Okay. Cool, but it would be fine if you were. I saw a woman scurrying off from this direction and I didn't know what to think."

I knew what to think. There was no reason to be by King's office unless it was to see him. There was literally nothing else around. I had a very bad feeling we'd been caught.

"It's nice to meet you, Pria. I'm Graham, a long-time friend of King's." He held out his hand and I robotically shook it as I internally freaked out.

"Oh, I didn't know he had any friends. You must be a good one." King pulled me to his side. His green eyes twinkled as he took me in. "I think we've been made." A somber expression fell over his face.

"So, what do you say to dinner? I can call Soraya and see if she wants to meet us. It can be a double date." Graham's face lit up with amusement. If I had to guess he'd never been on a double date in his life. Neither of them had.

"What do you say?" King squeezed my hip. "We

can go to Luciano's, eat good food, and have a couple of drinks to forget our troubles."

"Problems already?" Graham laughed as he started to head for the elevator as if it was a foregone conclusion we were going.

"We'll explain later. Maybe you can help us figure something out." King's tone held doubt as he ushered us to the elevator.

❀

"So, let me get this straight," Graham laughed before taking a sip of his scotch, "you're dating not only someone in Human Resources, but the director and you have a no fraternization policy at your company? You're fucked."

"Don't mind him." Soraya, Graham's beautiful girlfriend smiled at us with ruby red lips from across the table. Her long black hair was dyed blue at the ends and her big brown eyes were bright with happiness. "He's jaded to love in the workplace."

"Do you have any ideas? I'm pretty sure his secretary caught us tonight. She's been acting strange around me since I started back to work. Maybe she's had her suspicions." Looking over at King, I asked, "Did she act any different when you went back to work?" That could explain why she'd been an even bigger bitch.

"You took leave?" Graham's eyes lit up as if he'd landed on a juicy detail.

"At King's request. I was mugged two weeks ago and was pretty beat up." I lifted my casted arm. "My makeup is covering the bruises. You don't want to see what I look like underneath. I'm a walking—"

"Still beautiful." King kissed the top of my head.

"Hold up." Graham sat his drink down and clasped his hands together. "You took a vacation?"

"I wouldn't call it a vacation. I stayed home for a week to help Pria. Once she's better and I've got a break in my schedule, I'll go on a real vacation with her."

"You stayed home?" Graham asked in disbelief.

Soraya nudged him. "Be nice. You'd do the same for me. Why are you giving him such a hard time?"

Graham's eyes softened as he looked down at his girlfriend. "Of course, I'd do the same for you. I'd be at your beck and call for as long as you needed, but you don't know this guy. He's never been in a relationship or dated." His eyes got big as he looked back at King. "Ever."

"Yes, okay, we all get it," King deadpanned. "Why don't we focus on the problem of my secretary finding out about us."

"No one is going to take me seriously at my job if the person who's supposed to enforce the rules is breaking them." I buried my head in my hands. It wasn't as effective when one was covered with a cast, but I didn't care. I couldn't believe I'd already fucked this up.

"What if you said that if people did date they had to sign some form stating they were in a relationship and make rules about not dating someone who's directly under you so there's no nepotism?" Soraya shrugged.

"That's not a bad idea."

It wasn't a great one either. Maybe if the policy had been in place beforehand, but now it was like we were making rules so we could do whatever we wanted.

"Now I probably can't fire her, or she'll sue me," King growled out before he drained the rest of his drink.

"You should have filed a complaint," I added. Instead, he took on the work she hadn't been doing.

"Life is never boring with you." Graham laughed.

King laced our fingers together. A look of worry crossed his handsome face. "Right now, I wish it was, but whatever happens we'll get through this."

I only hoped he was right.

22
___

KINGSTON

G<small>OING BY THE LOOK ON EVERYONE'S FACE AS</small> I <small>WALKED</small> the distance from the elevator to my office, it was safe to say everyone knew about me and Pria. I wasn't sure how I was going to keep from firing my fucking secretary. Her time with Avery Capital Holdings was limited. If she filed a folder wrong, I was going to fire her ass.

Normally, I was the first one to work, but I had an early meeting out of the office that prevented me from appraising the situation. I hoped Pria wasn't getting the side looks and snickers I was getting. One look and they all cast their eyes down and went back to work. Last night, after we got home, she had slumped down on the couch and deteriorated before my eyes. I didn't care what anyone thought about me. They all already thought I was an asshole, but I understood why Pria felt the way she did. No one wanted to be known as the one who fucked their way up the ladder, and it would make her job difficult if no one took her seriously.

The problem was once it was out there, I couldn't do anything about it. The rumors had started, and they wouldn't stop anytime soon. If we had come out as a couple before someone heard us fucking in my office, it might have changed the way they looked at us. But no one wanted to announce to the world they were in a relationship until they knew it was going to last or out of its infancy.

I typed out a quick message to Pria.

KING: YOU SHOULD PROBABLY STAY IN YOUR OFFICE today.

Pria: Too late.

King: I'm sorry my dick got us in trouble. You can work from home until this blows over.

I KNEW AS I TYPED IT, IT WOULDN'T BLOW OVER ANYTIME soon, but I wanted to shelter her from the scrutiny. I knew if I caught anyone saying anything bad about her, I would likely fire them. I guess it was a good thing the head of my HR department didn't let me fire people for such things.

• • •

Pria: So you're saying for me to never come back?

King: All I can say is I'm sorry and I'll try to fix this mess.

Pria: I know you are, but you can't fix it.

King: I guess I shouldn't ask you to lunch?

Those three little bubbles appeared showing that she was typing. They went away and came back a couple of times before a new message finally showed up.

Pria: I'd love to have lunch with you.

King: Meet me downstairs at 11:30 and we'll hit this amazing sandwich place I know of that's not too far from here.

Pria: See you then.

That was easier than I thought it would be. Maybe I could convince her to work from home the rest of the day while we were at lunch. But if she stopped coming to work wouldn't that mean they'd won? Even though I hated this for her, Pria wasn't weak and could handle them. That was her job.

A knock sounded and I didn't bother to look up

as my secretary (no use finding out what her name was now since she wouldn't be around much longer) opened the door and peeked her head inside.

"You have a package," she said timidly. Her hands twisted together as she waited for me to speak.

Lifting my head, my eyes narrowed at her. I hoped she could feel my wrath and realized how much she had fucked up going against me. I'd make sure she never worked at any credible office again once she was out of here.

Getting back to work, I hit send on my email. "Sign for it."

"I already did."

"Then bring it in and set it down over there on the table." It wasn't like it was the first time I'd gotten a package since she worked here. If she was trying to test the waters to see if I knew it was her who spilled the proverbial beans, she was doing a shitty job.

"Yes, sir." It was quiet for a few minutes when I felt someone looking at me. Glancing up, I saw her in the middle of my office, her eyes trained on me.

"Is there something else? I'm busy," I growled, dropping my pen to my desk.

"Is there anything else, Mr. Avery?"

Was she fucking kidding me? Now she wanted to somewhat do her job?

"Nothing." My tone was lethal as I said the one word.

"I can get you a cup of coffee or…" She trailed off, batting her heavily made up eyes at me.

Was my secretary flirting with me? Did she think I'd fuck any employee?

"As a matter of fact, I do have something for you to do." I smiled wickedly.

Sandy or Cindy, or you were about to lose your job whatever your name was licked her bright pink lips. My stomach rolled at her action. I was revolted she'd think it would be so easy to get into my pants. The only thing I wanted everyone to think about me was that I was an asshole who got the job done.

"Anything," she answered back breathlessly.

"I need all the information we have on Gainsworth printed out."

Her face screwed up in confusion. "Everything?"

"Yes, everything. I need it on my desk by the end of the day. Thank you," I dismissed her.

It wasn't anything I needed. It was busywork, penance for thinking I would ask her to suck my cock now or ever.

I felt her linger for a few moments before she finally left. Blowing out a heavy sigh, I tried to clear my head, but it was hard to rein in my temper. I was mostly mad at myself for keeping her for as long as I had. I should have given her one warning after she didn't do her job the first time and after she failed again, gave her her walking papers with a smile on my face. Now, I was sure if I fired her, I'd be sued by the end of the week. My lawyers could handle it, but I didn't want Pria's name dragged through the mud.

I kept busy going through all the information I'd received on my trips and decided if I wanted to expand my business to California. Now that I had Pria in my life, I wasn't sure I wanted to make more work for myself. I wanted to be able to take time off and enjoy life. Something I hadn't done in a long time and wouldn't be able to do if I expanded my company.

Putting my computer to sleep, I grabbed my cell phone and headed to the elevator. This time as I passed through the halls everyone kept their heads down. There were no whispers or side glances, which gave me hope that they'd forgotten about Pria and me. Logically, I knew they hadn't, but I was still hopeful.

As I rode the elevator down to the lobby, I checked my phone for any messages, but aside from the hundred emails, I needed to answer there was nothing. When the elevator doors opened, I scanned the lobby looking for my lunch date. Since we were going a little early to beat the business lunch crowd, the only people in the lobby were security. A flash of black hair flowing in the wind caught my attention.

Pria was pacing outside. Upon further inspection, she was either talking to herself or was on the phone. Her hands flew as she spoke with her forehead creased with worry.

Guilt gnawed at me. Ever since Pria had come into my life, I'd caused her nothing but hardship. I hated it, but I wasn't willing to give her up. She was the best thing that had ever happened to me, and now it was up to me to figure out how I was going to be the best thing to come into her life.

Stepping in front of her to block her rapid back and forth, I reached out to pull my feisty girlfriend into my arms. Only she didn't come to me or greet me with anything but a paranoid look over her shoulder.

"Where's this sandwich place you were telling me about?"

I guess she hadn't been on the phone but talking to herself. Knowing that bit of information worried me. Had someone confronted her about us?

"Right this way." I pointed to the left and held my elbow out to her. With only a slight hesitation, she hooked her arm with mine and let me guide her down the busy sidewalk. We had been quiet since we'd left. I looked down at her as we waited to cross the road and wanted to kick myself in the ass. Her entire body was radiating worry and sadness. Why did people have to be assholes? Me included.

"Has anyone given you any trouble?"

"No one has even come into the department, but there's been plenty who've walked by gawking and whispering. It's like we're in high school." A heavy sigh deflated her already hunched posture. "I don't know what to do, King. I'm the laughingstock of the thirty-fourth floor."

Wrapping my arm around her shoulders, I pulled her into me and kissed the top of her head. "Give it a day or two for it to die down. If it doesn't, then…" I had no idea what I'd do, but I'd come up with something. Normally, I was good at thinking on the fly.

"Then what? Do you have any ideas, because I like my job and would like to keep it."

Wow. I stopped in my tracks at her words and stared down at her in shock. "You can't let them run you off. If you did, you're not the strong woman I know."

"Maybe I'm not the woman you know because right now that's the only option that makes sense."

"No, it doesn't make sense. Let's order our food and strategize. Between the two of us, surely we can come up with something that doesn't involve you leaving." I didn't want to think about what it would feel like for her to work somewhere else.

"Fine," she answered with no conviction in her voice.

Even though it was still a little early, the shop

was busy. While we waited in line to order, Pria stared down at her black peep toe heels with her hands clasped together in front of her. I kept the palm of my hand on the small of her back in a silent show of solidarity. I wracked my brain for ways for Pria to stay at Avery Capital Holdings and be taken seriously, but I wasn't sure how to do the latter. I couldn't make anyone respect her or listen to her, but I could make sure that anyone who didn't treat her like everyone else, would have it marked in their file and if it continued to happen, be fired. I didn't care if I had to hire an entire new staff.

We ordered our sandwiches. Mine a teriyaki chicken with bean sprouts and hers a ham and Swiss with water for us to drink. Their teriyaki chicken was what kept me coming back to the sandwich shop. I wasn't sure how they made it taste as amazing as they did, but I was addicted to it. Carrying our tray to an empty table, I sat across from Pria and took her in. Her eyes were downcast as she sat slumped in her seat. She was in a bad way, there was no doubt about it.

Handing her sandwich over, I opened mine and took a bite before I spoke. "I wish I had some magical words to make this all better, but I don't. If you want, I can fire everyone and let you hire an all new staff."

She bit the inside of her cheek before looking up

and rolled her eyes at me. "Don't be ridiculous. You can't do that, and I won't let you."

Taking another bite, I chewed and watched her pick at her sandwich. She pulled off a little piece and popped it in her mouth.

"We could do what Soraya mentioned. Why not supply a document and come out as a couple?"

She choked on her bite and coughed a few times. After taking a drink of her water, Pria sat up taller in her seat. "And what happens when we break up? Do I find a new job then?"

"What makes you think we'll break up? I thought after the night in the hospital that we... I don't know." I shrugged. I wasn't good at talking about my feelings or having feelings at all for that matter.

Her face softened. Reaching across the table for my hand, she clasped hers over mine. "We did. Sometimes I think it was all a dream or the drugs were playing tricks on me. I never thought I'd be your type. I mean look at you." She indicated my chest, but I didn't think it had anything to do with what she was talking about.

I sat back in my seat, my sandwich forgotten. "I don't understand. What did you think my type was?"

"You're a strange mix of the boy next door and a model who's extremely cocky, but somehow you make it work for you. It doesn't make sense but it's very appealing. You don't need to tell me how good-looking you are or how amazing your body is. I saw you with supermodels and ex-cheerleaders, and here I am this little Chinese girl."

I didn't need her to tell me, but I liked knowing how attracted she was to me.

"You're my type, Pria. I love how small and tight your body is. I love how we fit together, and I love how you don't take any of my shit. And you should know you could be a supermodel with how gorgeous you are."

She scoffed. "If I was like ten inches taller maybe."

"I don't care about your height. I know what I see."

"You sure know how to make a girl feel good when she's down. Who would have thought?"

"Certainly not me, but you've worked your way into my heart. I don't see what we have having an end date. I'd happily send out a memo to the entire staff declaring you're mine, but I understand if you don't want to."

"I hate this. I'm back for two days getting looks because of my arm and your secretary probably telling everyone I was in the hospital after I sent her that email, and now this."

There wasn't anything I could say to make her

feel better, so I stayed silent and tried to show my support by being there for her.

"Maybe it was too soon for me to come back," she murmured. "I could work from home, but I don't want them to think they can scare me off." Her eyes filled with tears and her chin trembled. "I don't know what to do, King."

"I say we make a united front and show there's nothing they can say or do that bothers us. You do your job and if anyone gives you a hard time, put it in their file and let them know. We do quarterly reviews on all our employees and they all know there's a three strikes and they're out policy. Next month everyone is up for review and I doubt they want to lose their jobs."

"Do you think it's that easy?"

"I don't know, is it? I don't care what they say about me, but if I hear them badmouthing you it will be the total opposite. But I sincerely doubt anyone is going to be saying anything around me. They know to be scared of me."

"It's a good thing you're a cocky asshole." She cracked a tight smile.

"Most days it is. Let's go in there and show them it's you and me, and we don't give a fuck what they say."

"That's easy for you to say."

It was.

"I'll do whatever will make this easier for you, but you're a fighter and a hard-ass bitch when it comes to your job. If you weren't, I wouldn't have hired you."

Wrapping her sandwich up, she picked up her water bottle. "Thank you, I needed to hear that. Let's go kick their asses."

All right, I guess we were doing this.

23

KINGSTON

Pria smiled up at me as we broke apart, but it didn't meet her eyes. It had only been two weeks since everyone at Avery Capital Holdings heard rumors about us and then we came out. If coming out was stepping off the elevator holding hands and me giving her a light kiss as we went our separate ways.

I'd filled out the paperwork stating we were a couple and so had Pria, so I wasn't sure what was happening with her. Every time I asked her how her day was she said it was fine, but I knew it was anything but. Whitmore had come to my office and informed me of the rumors about Pria and me. None of them were good and to make matters worse, my secretary continued to flirt with me every chance she got. Pria and I had been having lunch in my office every day (with no sex, much to my disappointment) and I had a feeling she'd caught Sandy flirting with me one of the days when she brought in our lunch. Pria hadn't mentioned it, but it did seem to make her pull away more.

The only good thing that had happened was my secretary had started to do more of the work she should have been doing from the moment she started working here. Little did she know, nothing she could do would put her in my good graces. She would be fired, it was only a matter of when.

Not only was Pria dealing with the bullshit at the office, but she'd been helping her new friend, Aubrey, with the event that was coming up at the end of the week. Even as busy as she was, Pria had been going to bed early and sleeping in every morning. It left us little time outside of the workplace and we barely saw each other at work, to begin with. That's why I had started having lunch with her every day in my office.

I wasn't sure if she was depressed about work, if she was pulling away because she was planning on ending things with me, or if it was something else. Whatever it was, I was afraid I was losing her when I'd only just gotten her.

Pria

THE MOMENT I STEPPED INTO THE FUNDRAISER, AUBREY grabbed me by my arm and dragged me into the corner. Her green eyes scrutinized my down-turned face. "Are things still not better at work?" I'd told her everything hoping for advice from an outside source. Things had gotten somewhat better, but there were still people whispering and snickering as I walked by. I couldn't tell King about it. His solution was for me to fire anyone who made me uncomfortable and I couldn't do that. It wasn't all bad. There were a few who said King was tolerable now that I'd come into his life and thanked me for it.

"Today I didn't even notice." Tears stung my eyes and I bit my bottom lip. "My grandmother is in the hospital. Sadly, we haven't gotten along since I left to go to college and now, I don't know if I'll ever get the chance to talk to her."

Aubrey's mouth open and closed. She gave me a side hug. "I'm so sorry."

"Thank you. I just want to talk to her and try and get her approval even though I know no matter how hard I try I'll never get it."

"Why not?" she asked softly.

"My family is very traditional, especially my Lao Lao." At her confused face, I explained. "That's what I call my grandmother. She thought I should get married and stay home instead of going to college and working. I've been avoiding her since I found my ex-fiancé fucking someone on our kitchen table and moved out."

"I'm so sorry, Pria. I didn't know. I would have understood if you wanted to skip out on tonight."

"This is a nice distraction from everything going on in my life. When I've helped you, I forget about my problems and that's a nice change."

"While it might be nice to run away from your problems for a little while, what are you going to do? Have you talked to your boyfriend? What does he have to say?"

"Nothing because I haven't talked to him. While he's sweet to me, he can be a real asshole and his solution at work is to fire anyone who even looks at me wrong. I've been keeping it to myself and being a pretty bad girlfriend. I've decided, though, that I'm not going to let them get to me. I love my job and I can't imagine not seeing King every day. Ever since we came out, he's cleared his lunch schedule so we can have lunch with each other."

"He sounds like a good guy."

"Surprisingly, he is. At first, I thought he was a cocky asshole."

Aubrey stifled a giggle. "They do seem to make a bad first, second, and third impression, and then they surprise us. By the way, where is he? I thought he was going to be your date. I was hoping to meet him so I could thank him for his generous contribution."

"He should be here soon. He had something come up and I wanted to stop by the hospital to see if there was any change in my grandmother, so we came separately. I want to thank you for being a good friend these last couple of weeks and talking me down from the ledge."

"You don't have to thank me. In fact, I should be the one thanking you for helping me with everything. I'm not sure the night would be a success without your organization skills and the money you brought in from Avery Capital Holdings and Morgan Financial Holdings. That money is going to go a long way to our cause."

I was surprised when King and I were at dinner with Graham and his girlfriend, Soraya, and Graham had said he'd match the amount King was donating. They planned on coming, but Graham's daughter Chloe was sick, and she wanted both Graham and Soraya by her side. I thought it was adorable.

A tall and very handsome man with thick brown hair pulled Aubrey to his chest. "There you are. You're a hard woman to find." I was shocked to hear an Australian accent. Aubrey hadn't mentioned it in all the times we talked.

She swatted at his hand that rested on her stomach. "Stop. You knew exactly where to find me." She looked over her shoulder at him and her eyes glittered with happiness. "Chance, I want you to meet my friend, Pria. She's the one I told you about, who has been helping me with tonight."

He smiled at me and a set of dimples popped out. I nearly swooned on the spot. I'd never met anyone with dimples and now I knew their true effect on women. Aubrey was one lucky lady. Disentangling one hand, he held it out for me to shake. "It's nice to meet you, Pria."

"It's nice to meet you too."

Aubrey's eyes lit up as she looked over my shoulder. "There's a blond god walking this way with his eyes set on you. Is it your boss?" A knowing smirk grew on her face.

I turned to see King striding toward me with an air of confidence that only he could make look natural. He was decked out in a form fitting tuxedo that had my jaw hitting the floor. When he noticed me taking him in, a cocky smile spread across his face.

He didn't stop until I was in his arms, one hand resting low on my back. "You look absolutely radiant tonight."

"Thank you. You cleaned up nicely yourself." I'd never seen King in a tux, and it made me want to jump him in front of everyone or find a bathroom to have a quickie in. It didn't help that it had been a few days since he was last inside me. Every day at lunch, he tried unsuccessfully to get me naked.

"Will you dance with me?" The uncertainty in his eyes made my heartache. I hadn't been handling the situation at work well, and I was taking it out on King. The news about my Lao Lao being in the hospital only added to it. I hadn't even mentioned it to King yet. At first, I was still processing the fact I'd likely never speak to her again, and then King had been busy at work. I needed to tell him, but I wanted to enjoy this moment with him first.

Placing my hand in his, I gave it a squeeze. With that touch alone, I was already calmer. "I'd love nothing more than to dance with you."

King pulled me out onto the makeshift dance floor. Our bodies pressed together in a lovers' embrace. I didn't even know if we matched the music the band was playing, but I didn't care. I was lost in King's eyes. In the dark room, they looked like sparkling emeralds that held so many unnamed emotions in them.

Bringing his forehead to mine, King looked down at me with pain in his eyes. "I don't know what's going on between us, but I've missed you even with you right by my side."

"I know none of this makes sense and I'm sorry." I rested my hand over his heart. "I've missed you too. I'm sorry I've been distant. It's not fair to you. I want to talk, but not tonight. Tonight, I want to enjoy my gorgeous boyfriend in his tux."

"Have I done something—"

I cut him off with a finger to his full lips. "You've been perfect. I promise you, it's all me."

"I know I'm no good at this boyfriend stuff, but when you're ready to talk, I'm here."

My hand ran up his chest and cupped the side of his neck. "You're pretty perfect, if you ask me."

Even in the dark, I could see King's eyes light up. His hold on me tightened as he pulled me deeper into his body. "I love you." His eyes widened before he dipped down and caressed his lips against mine. "That wasn't very smooth, was it?" He laughed uncomfortably.

"The fact that it wasn't, shows me how much you really mean it." I was sure King had never told anyone but his family that he loved them since he'd never been in a relationship, and now he loved me. It was mind-blowing and made me love him all the more.

Wrapping both my hands around his neck or as best as I could with one in a cast, I stretched up on my toes even though I had on high heels to whisper against his lips. "Never in my wildest dreams did I think it would be possible, but I love you too." King took control, slipping his tongue into my mouth and curled it along mine. My heart rate picked up and I wanted nothing more than to be alone with him.

Pulling back, King chuckled against my mouth.

"You're vibrating, and I don't think it's me causing it."

I was? I was too wrapped up in King that I hadn't noticed my purse vibrating until it started again. Coming back to reality, I pulled out my phone to see my father calling. My heart plummeted into my stomach. It could only mean one thing. My grandmother.

Reaching up, I kissed him before pulling away. "I'm sorry, King. I've got to go."

I left him standing there in the middle of the dance floor with furrowed brows and swollen lips.

24

PRIA

T<small>EARS STREAMED DOWN MY FACE AS</small> I <small>STARED AT THE</small> dirt covered ground. My father's hand squeezed my shoulder. "Sweetheart, she wouldn't want you to be sad."

"I don't know about that," I choked out. "I can't remember the last time we got along. She hated that Haider and I hadn't gotten married yet or that she wasn't a great-grandmother."

"While she did want those things, she also wanted you to be happy. It was hard for her to admit, but she was proud of you. Of how much you fought for what you believed in. I'm proud of you too even though I don't say it often."

Sniffing, I wiped my tears with the back of my hand. "Do you really mean that?"

"Of course, I do." He closed his eyes as a fleeting look of pain shot across his face. "When I came to see you at work the other day and saw how happy it makes you, it made me realize I shouldn't push my beliefs on you. You've always been your own person and I should have accepted that long ago instead of pushing you away. I want you to be happy, and up until recently, you haven't been. I think your Lao Lao, me, and Haider had a big part in that. Something's new and it's making you truly smile for the first time since you went off to college. Is it your new job or something else?"

The thought of King brought a calm to me that hadn't been there since I found out my grandmother died. I missed him, but I'd asked him to stay away unsure of how my family would react to him being at the funeral. He wasn't happy, but he understood I needed to come by myself. No one knew of my white boyfriend, and I didn't want to start any drama, but my dad had asked so I wasn't going to lie to him.

I shifted on the bench to look at him. "It's something else, or I guess I should say someone else. It wasn't planned."

"It rarely is, honey. Why didn't you tell me about him when we had lunch?" He looked around the cemetery with his hand shielding his eyes. It was bright out and it seemed all wrong for the mood I was in. It should be gray and cold. "Why didn't he accompany you to the funeral?"

"Because I asked him not to. I wasn't sure how

well it would go over if my tall, blond, and American boyfriend showed up and sat beside me." I bit my bottom lip waiting for my father's response.

"I give you an inch and you take a mile." My father chuckled next to me as he stared down at the cold broken dirt in front of us. "Does he treat you right? Better than Haider?"

I smiled to myself at the possibility that King might be accepted easier than I thought by my family. Maybe I should have introduced him to my Lao Lao. He might have charmed the pants off her.

"He treats me better than any man ever has. I didn't plan on King coming into my life the way he did."

"King? What kind of name is that?"

"You know him, father. His name is Kingston Avery. He offered me a place to stay after what happened with Haider and—"

"You should have come home." He barked as he stood up and looked down at me. Rapid fire Chinese spat out of his mouth as he paced in front of me. I wasn't fluent, but I caught some of what he was saying and none of it was good.

He was very disappointed that I jumped from living with one man to another while unmarried. It wouldn't have been any better if I had been married, but I understood what he was saying. I was a disgrace in his eyes.

His brown eyes so much like my own filled with disappointment and his mouth opened and closed, but in the end, he chose to walk away.

HOURS LATER A LARGE BODY SAT DOWN BESIDE ME AND I bristled. I wanted to be left alone and didn't want to deal with anyone invading my privacy. When a warm arm rested across my shoulders, I nearly shot up from my seat. Turning to fight with whoever was there to bother me, I was surprised to find King. He was clad in one of his many ten-thousand-dollar suits with sunglasses hiding his eyes. "What are you doing here?" My voice came out as a croak after many hours of not speaking.

King gave me a sad smile. "Your dad called me."

"My dad? How?" He'd left hours ago, and more importantly, why had he called King?

"I'm not really sure. He said something about how you were upset and had been sitting here for hours. I asked him where you were and left immediately to come to you." His large hand covered mine that were clasped in my lap. "I'm sorry you had to go through this alone. You know I would have been here for you if you would have let me."

Leaning my head on his shoulder, I snuggled into his side wrapping my arm around his trim waist. The heat radiating off him soothed my body that had chilled after hours of sitting outside. With King by my side, the death of my grandmother and the rejection of my father didn't hurt as much anymore. "I know you would have. I didn't want to rock the boat, but I ended up doing it anyway. I told my father about you."

"So, I'm no longer your dirty little secret." He gave me a squeeze to let me know he was joking. Only I wasn't sure if he was really joking about it or if some small part of him felt like I wanted to keep the fact that he was my boyfriend hidden from the world.

Pulling back enough to be able to look up at him, I held his gaze. I wanted him to know how I truly felt. "You were never my secret, even when I didn't want the world to know about us. You were always my prize."

"Shorty, you don't have to reassure me. I'm here for you, not the other way around." His icy green eyes twinkled at me.

"What was your plan to make me feel better? Were you going to whisk me away or let your dog's kiss me into submission?" I had to admit to myself some puppy kisses would help. Jimmy and Orvy always seemed to know what I needed. I never knew dogs could be so tuned into the humans they were around.

"All good plans, but I had something different in mind." He sat up straighter and ran his hand through his already ruffled but sexy hair. "Do you remember the other night when I said I had something to do before the fundraiser?"

"Yes, of course, I do. I thought it was strange since we planned on going together and then out of nowhere you changed the plans."

King smiled nervously. I could see his pulse pick up in his neck and I instantly got nervous, afraid I'd lost him when I pushed him away. Maybe it was because I made him feel less than regarding my family. All I knew was that I'd be devastated if my stupid actions cost me the best thing that had ever happened to me.

He cleared his throat, his grip on me tightening. "I had other plans for us that night." My face fell. My heart dropped into my stomach and broke shattering into a million pieces as I stared back at him. "Christ, I'm doing this all wrong." King tugged at his hair. "You don't need to worry. Like I've told you before, I suck at expressing myself unless I'm pissed off." His free hand fished in his pocket for a long moment before he pulled out a keyring. King shifted until we were facing each other with our legs pressed together. "This is what I wanted to do the other night." He held out the keyring. "I know this might seem early in our relationship, but when you know you know. I want to wake up with you by my side and fall asleep wrapped around you. What do you say?"

All of that just to ask me to live with him? "I'm not going anywhere, and I already have a key. You didn't need to get me a key chain to make it official."

"That's not..." King held the key chain up until it was directly in my eyesight. "I don't want you to live with me." Amusement shone in his voice. "I want you to marry me, Pria Wang."

"You want to marry me?" My ears must have been playing tricks on me. Who asked someone to marry them by giving them a keyring?

"I know you're the one for me. We can have a long engagement, get married at the courthouse, or run off to Vegas and elope. Whatever you want, but please tell me that you want to spend the rest of your life with me."

King's words knocked the breath out of me. Throwing my arms around his broad shoulders, I peppered kisses all over his gorgeous face. "Since the moment you let me in," I placed my hand over his rapidly beating heart, "you've made me happier than I've ever been. I can't wait to wake up with you by my side."

The smile that broke across King's face would forever be cemented in my heart. His warm hands cupped my face as he dipped low and slid his tongue ever so slowly along the seam of my upturned lips. I opened for him, my fingers threading through his hair as I soaked in the moment. My heart was about ready to beat out of my chest. I couldn't believe this was my life. That King would be mine for the rest of my days. His hand curled around mine as the other slid to the back of my neck and held me. Deepening the kiss, we groaned and let ourselves get lost in the moment.

Pulling back, his thumb caressed my cheek.

"But why a key chain? Is this some new tradition you're starting?"

Kissing me again only this time shorter, King shook the set of keys. "I was afraid I'd lose it, so I clipped it on my keys. Probably not the smartest move, but I thought you'd see it." Unsure of how I hadn't managed to see the ring that glittered in the light, I gasped. King quickly unclipped it and held it out for me to see. It was a large sapphire with diamonds on the side. It was perfect and what I would have picked out for myself if given the chance.

"It's beautiful and perfect." Tears stung the backs of my eyes. I blinked to clear my vision but was unsuccessful. The moment was so unexpected and wonderful I couldn't contain my happy tears. Even though his method had been unconventional, I knew I'd never forget that day.

25

PRIA

Epilogue

I'D BEEN SITTING IN THE SAME SPOT FOR THE LAST THIRTY minutes in shock. As the door swung open, I blinked up at my husband.

King's laser green eyes scanned the bathroom before landing on me, and his eyes instantly softened. I loved the look that came over his face every time he looked at me. The love that emanated from him truly astounded me sometimes. Who would have ever thought the cocky, ten-thousand-dollar suit wearing Kingston Avery would be a softy underneath all the assholeness he exuded? One who at home shed the suits for T-shirts and sweatpants. While I loved seeing him in his suits there was nothing sexier than seeing him wearing a pair of gray sweatpants riding low on his hips showcasing his impressive V.

"What have you been doing in here? Dinner's getting cold. I thought you were starving after volunteering all day at the animal shelter."

"I'm not sure I can eat dinner tonight." My hands trembled.

He cocked his head to the side. "But it's from your favorite Italian restaurant."

Tears welled in my eyes and my chin quivered. "I know, but I'm not feeling good." I rested a hand on my fluttering stomach.

King knelt down in front of me. His throat bobbed as he took me in. "Don't cry. I can put your food in the refrigerator if you don't want to eat it tonight. Whatever you want." Even after all this time together, my tears still made him uncomfortable.

I sat quietly, unsure how to process what was happening. King's warm hands ran up my calves to then rest on my knees. "Please, tell me what's going on with you. This isn't like you." His eye begged me to start talking.

"You did it. After having sex for the millionth time, you defied the odds and got me pregnant." I held the pregnancy test out for him to see.

King shook his head and a bright smile spread across his handsome face as he looked down at the plus sign. "If I was defying the odds as you put it, I would have gotten you pregnant a long time ago." His smile dropped off his face as sad eyes looked up at me. Instead of a light green, they turned into a dark green that made my heart race. "Are you not happy about this? I thought..." He shook his head as if he had no more words.

"I didn't think it would happen so fast. After being on birth control for over a decade I thought it would take at least a year. I thought Prada would be potty trained. Why did we have to get Jimmy a girl-friend?" We'd both learned it wasn't as easy as we thought to potty train a dog. Orvy, Sarah, and Jimmy had already been trained for the most part before King got them. I thought the exhaustion I'd been feeling for the last couple of weeks was from getting up so many times during the night to let Prada out, and King keeping me up late at night, but when I started to feel nauseated earlier, I decided to see if by some off chance I might be pregnant.

"Would you listen to yourself?" He barked out a laugh. The sadness in his eyes now turned into amusement. "The baby isn't coming today or tomor-row. By the time he or she is here, Prada will be potty trained. I promise. I will make it my mission to make your life—"

Placing my finger to his lips, I couldn't help it as my lips tipped up. I wanted to laugh, but I held back. "You, Kingston Avery, give me the best life possible. I love you and I can't wait to have this baby with you. I know you're going to be the best dad ever." A tear slipped down my cheek.

Leaning in, King kissed away my lone tear. "Shorty, you've given me the best gift ever. Thank you. Now I think I'd like to give you one more gift." A sexy smirk made one side of his kissable mouth lift. His hands slipped under my legs as he pulled me closer until our chest were flush. My legs wrapped around his trim waist bringing our centers into contact. "Is it bad that I'm turned on right now?"

I ground my clit against the seam of his jeans and moaned. "If it is then I'm bad right along with you. I need to feel you inside of me."

King's brows dipped. "Are you sure it's safe? I don't want to plow into the baby."

"Are you kidding me?" I broke out laughing and face planted into his chest. "Please don't tell me you're planning to withhold sex from me for the next however many months." I would die and King would explode. Even after being married for three years, I was still addicted to my gorgeous husband. In fact, I found him sexier now than when we met.

"I could never deny you my cock for that long." He rubbed said length along my jean clad pussy.

"Always a gentleman." I moaned.

Picking me up off the counter, he turned around and took us straight to our bed. It was still unmade from our earlier romp this morning. Laying me down gently, he pulled my jeans down my legs before he slipped my shirt over my head leaving me in only my bra and panties. King hovered over me. His gaze traveled down my body and darkened with lust with each inch he took in.

"You get more beautiful each day." His large hand ran up my thigh and skated over where I wanted it most to splay over my stomach. "I can't wait to see you round with my child. Everyone will know you're mine."

Bringing my left hand up, I waved it in front of him. "You think this ring doesn't do its job? Or the way you growl at anyone who so much as looks at me when we're at work or on the street."

King lowered himself until he was settled between my hips. His brows pinched together. "Those assholes deserve it after the way they treated you when they found out about us."

"It's been three years and they're not assholes now."

Almost everyone had changed their tune once they saw that we were serious about infractions being put in their files. After King's secretary was caught banging one of the employees that had kept sneering at me in the bathroom, she was promptly fired and King had never been happier.

"Because they're scared for their jobs and rightfully so. Why are we talking about work? I want to make love to my wife after hearing that my super-hero sperm did the unthinkable and got her pregnant."

I couldn't help but laugh until I felt his hardened length press against me. "Why do you still have clothes on?" I retorted as I ran my hands under his T-shirt.

"Good question, Mrs. Avery." King hopped up off the bed and took his clothes off so fast you'd think he was on fire. I wanted to laugh, but as each garment was thrown to the floor my body heated in anticipation of what would come next. In the blink of an eye, he had removed his clothes and took the liberty of ridding me of the rest of mine as well.

Starting at the foot of the bed, King prowled up the bed like a lion after its prey. I licked my lips as I watched his cock bob with every movement. I wanted to feel it in my hands, wrap my mouth around it and taste his saltiness, and feel it stretch me as he pumped inside me. His large hands trailed up the inside of my thighs as he bent down and licked a path from my knee to the edge of my hip. I squirmed wanting to feel his tongue along my slit or better yet tapping my clit.

My husband grinned up at me as if he knew exactly what I was thinking before he repeated the same action only this time when he reached the apex of my thighs, his hands grabbed my hips to hold me in place as his thumbs spread my lips open. His skilled tongue swiped through my slit and up to my clit where he swirled and sucked on it until I was a writhing mess. Dipping down he fucked me with his tongue. My back tried to arch off the bed, but his hands kept me in place. Plunging my fingers into his blond locks, I tried to direct him where I wanted him, but King wasn't having any of it. He only shook his head as he repeated his torture of gliding his tongue up and down my swollen lips to then attack my bundle of nerves until I was about ready to explode, only to then start all over again.

I growled out my frustration. King looked up at me with my juices covering his mouth and chin, a sexy smile on his face. "You sound like a kitten. Are you not liking what I'm doing?" His devilish grin told me he knew exactly how much I was enjoying it and what I wanted.

"Yes, but I want more," I whined as I tried to thrust my hips up. "Please," I begged without shame. If he was in a mood, King might draw my orgasm out until I was blue in the face.

"Since you asked so nicely." His voice was husky and full of sex. He was wound up and needing release just as much as I was. Leaning down, he gave me one last lick before he attached his lips to my clit and sucked hard.

I bowed off the mattress. My head thrashed back and forth as heat shot down my spine and straight to where his mouth covered me.

Letting go of my hip, King pinched one nipple and then the other as his tongue licked, swirled and tapped sending me over the edge. My thighs shook and fell open to give him better access. With one final twist of his tongue, he crawled up my body leaving kisses in his wake.

Once firmly seated between my legs, he slid his length up and down my slick folds and tapped my bud at the end. Placing his cock at my entrance, he pushed in with one hard thrust. We both moaned as my walls contracted around him. Grabbing both my hands in his, King positioned them above my head and laced our fingers together. His hips started to move slowly at first. Rocking into me with his pelvis hitting my already sensitive bundle of nerves. My second orgasm started to build quickly.

"Squeeze me harder." He groaned as his movements picked up speed. I tightened my inner muscles around his length, bringing another long moan from his lips.

He pulled back and thrust into me all the while his eyes never leaving mine. His hips pounded into mine as he chased his pleasure. The grip of his hands pressed me farther into the bed. He was close and so was I.

Bringing my legs up higher on his waist, I clenched around him as I felt him start to swell and pulse inside of me. With one final thrust, King pressed the base of his cock into my clit and rotated his hips. My core pulsed around him as fire licked up my body.

King moaned into my mouth before he plunged his tongue deep inside as I milked his length. I caressed his tongue with mine until we broke apart panting. Giving me one last kiss, King fell to the side and brought me with him making me lay slanted across him. Our hearts beat against each other's in the same fast rhythm.

After several long moments, I leaned down and kissed his chest above his heart. "If I wasn't already pregnant that would have done it."

"I agree." He hummed before his body stiffened. I felt him turn before he reached down and pulled the blankets up and over us. He grumbled under his breath. "Oh, for fuck's sake, Sarah, stop staring. She touched her cold-ass nose to my ass."

She was probably trying to stake her claim on King. We still weren't the best of friends, but most of the time she listened to me. I looked to the other side of the bed and nudged King in the side. "Maybe you should tell Jimmy to stop humping his bed."

Looking over, King laughed, but his eyes quickly came back to me. "His bed is a whole lot safer than little Prada. Let's let him have his fun. I think he's jealous." If I thought Jimmy was small, Prada was tiny since she was only three months old.

"That's gross and probably true." I slid off his side as I laughed. "We really need to start locking the door since Orvy opens it for the rest of them to come in."

"Where's the fun in that?" The laughter in his voice made me smile. "Did you ever think you'd love them as much as you do when you first came here?"

Turning back into his arms, I rested my chin on my husband's shoulder. "I was just as surprised with them as I was you. Who knew what a blessing in disguise me not having any place to live would be?"

"We've had one hell of a ride, haven't we? At least your dad talks to me now." He chuckled low in his throat as his eyes lit up. "Maybe not now that I've impregnated his daughter."

Resting my head back down, my fingers traced shapes along his chest. "I have no doubt he'll love him or her. Plus, he's got a few months to get used to the idea."

"Do you know how far along you are?"

"I'm not sure. I'm going to call my ob-gyn tomorrow and make an appointment. We'll find out then." I chewed on the inside of my lip as I contemplated saying what I was about to say. "King?" I propped my head on my hand and looked down at him.

"Yeah, shorty?"

"I've been thinking since I stopped taking my birth control about what we'd name our child and I was thinking of naming him or her Murphy. What do you think?"

King's eyes became glassy as his gaze captured mine. His Adam's apple bobbed as he tried to speak and failed. After a few seconds, he pulled himself together and pulled me into a crushing hug as he peppered kisses all over my face, neck, and collarbone.

"I think that's the best idea you've had since you agreed to be mine."

"Yeah? It doesn't upset you?" I knew how much King loved his sister and I couldn't think of a better way to honor her than to name our first child after her.

"Upset me? No, I can't think of a better way to celebrate her life than naming our child after her. I'm sure she would have come up with something crazy if she were here, but I believe she'd approve." His head dipped and he brushed his lips to mine in a gentle kiss. "Thank you for thinking of her."

I had no words. Instead, I pulled King into a hug and let him bury his face into my neck. After all these years, it was still his favorite place to be besides between my legs.

It was sad Murphy lost her life so young, and the girl I remembered had always been so happy and carefree, even though she was sick and bedridden much of the times I saw her. This was the least I could do for a wonderful woman and the man I loved. I knew Murphy would have gotten a kick out of King and I being together.

King's hand caressed up my back. "What do you say we practice making baby number two? Maybe I can still break a record and get you pregnant while you're already pregnant."

Sitting up so I was straddling him, I playfully swatted at him. "That's impossible, but maybe you can break your record for the number of orgasms you can give me in twenty-four hours."

He grinned at the idea. Nothing made my husband happier than bringing me pleasure. "How about we call in sick tomorrow? I'll put in a good word with your boss, so you don't get fired."

"I think my boss would approve if he knew what I was doing."

Aligning his cock to my entrance, King pushed in. "Agreed."

~ The End ~

COCKY HERO CLUB

Want to keep up with all of the new releases in Vi Keeland and Penelope Ward's Cocky Hero Club world? Make sure you sign up for the official Cocky Hero Club newsletter for all the latest on our upcoming books: https://www.subscribepage.com/CockyHeroClub

http://www.cockyheroclub.com

ACKNOWLEDGMENTS

My family- your support means so much. Thank you for all of your encouragement and giving me the time to do what makes me happy.

To **my girls**: QB Tyler , Carmel Rhodes, Kelsey Cheyenne, Melissa Spence Erica Marselas, Danielle James, Rose Croft, Helen Wilder, Gemini Jensen, and Alexis Rae. I love each and every one of you. Thank you for all of your support.

Kelly: I don't know what I'd do without you. Thank you for EVERYTHING you did you cheer me on while I wrote this book and kept me on track!

Thank you **Kristen Breanne** for making my story into a book.

To all my **author friends**, you know who you are. Thank you for accepting me and making me feel welcome in this amazing community.

To **Vi Keeland** and **Penelope Ward,** thank you for giving me this amazing opportunity to write in a world that I've loved for years.

Lovers thank you for always being there.

To each and every **reader, reviewer,** and **blog** - I would be nowhere without you. Thank you for taking a chance on an unknown author.

ABOUT HARLOW

Harlow Layne is a contemporary romance author who loves to write sexy alphas that will make you swoon and feisty heroines that will make you want to be their best friend.

Harlow wrote fanfiction for years before she decided to write Luke and Alex's story that had been swimming in her head for years.

When Harlow's not writing you'll find her online shopping on Amazon, Facebook, or Instagram or hanging out with her family and two dogs.

ALSO BY HARLOW LAYNE

Fairlane Series

With Love, Alex

Hollywood Redemption

Hollywood Fairytale

Unsteady in Love

Kiss Me

Standalones

Intern

Secret Admirer

The Model

Anthologies

Spiced Holiday Kisses

Risking Everything Anthology

Made in the USA
Monee, IL
19 September 2020